30 TO 50
FERAL HOGS

PRAISE FOR 30 TO 50 FERAL HOGS

"Action-packed and relentless. Ingram has summoned the bloody spawn of *The Descent*, *The Grey*, and a mess of angry swine. One wild gauntlet of a book."

- Hailey Piper, author of *A Light Most Hateful*

"One of those books that's exactly what you hope it would be when you first see it: fun, frequently hilarious, and action-packed. What you don't expect is that it's also packed with feelings, real people dealing with their very real issues and past, an adorable dog buddy that stole my heart, and, most surprisingly, sexual tension through the roof. A real treat of a read for when you're feeling blue and like the 30 to 50 feral hogs of life might be about to get you down."

- Alex Woodroe, author of *Whisperwood*

"Ingram has written one of the more fun, untamed October romps. Broken readers will indulge in the struggles of these women hunting not only feral hogs but a higher purpose: hunting their real selves (albeit, selves covered in grime, blood, and bruises)."

- Steve Berman, Lambda Literary Award-winning editor of *His Seed*

ALSO BY DAYNA INGRAM

FROM LETHE PRESS

The Golden Daughter
All Good Children
Eat Your Heart Out

Sleep Like This

30 TO 50 FERAL HOGS

DAYNA INGRAM

Cover and Illustrations by
Tom Bagley

THE SEVENTH TERRACE

30 to 50 Feral Hogs

Copyright © 2023 Dayna Ingram

30 to 50 Feral Hogs
ISBN 13: 978-1-990082-26-9
First Trade Paperback Edition - 2023

Cover and Illustrations © 2023 Tom Bagley

The Seventh Terrace
www.the-seventh-terrace.com

For Myles, who is always in my corner.

Chapter One

As Parker Eriksen pried yet another tooth out of her bloody maw, she thought again about quitting. Getting out of this podunk mountain backwater and returning to civilization. The thought chased the shot of liquor across her tongue and she gargled both, spitting them into the grimy sink. She watched her cracked tooth circle the drain in a swirl of Knob Creek, and knew she'd never quit. Never run back to where she came from, or to any other place for that matter. This was the place she'd run to when shit went sour. This was the hole where she'd buried herself. What was the point in digging up what was already dead?

She fished the tooth out of the sink and chucked it into the waste bin, along with the greasy rag she'd used to sop up her blood. By the dim light of the bulb swinging in the wood-paneled bathroom, she looked herself over in the spit-stained mirror. Not quite dead yet, on the outside, but looking mighty similar.

Parker had never been pretty by a long stretch. She'd near about broken and re-healed every bone in her face over the years, which didn't help matters. These days, she chopped her own soul-dark locks into a dismal imitation of a pixie cut— didn't want to give anyone something to grab. No earrings for the same reason, although the holes she'd punched in her lobes as a teenager never did close up. She was tall and large, all meat, gristle and bone. Scarred and sun-bleached and gap-toothed. She held a finger to the nostril of her crooked nose and shot a clot of filmy green boogers onto the mirror. One more fight to go.

Jimmy's Gym. A locker room with a couple of church pews hacksawed into benches, milk crates piled together against a window-less wall, full to bursting with towels and tees and socks that were desperate for a wash. The stamping feet of the impatient crowd out in the gym proper vibrated the concrete floor. Their drunken bellows echoed into the hollow space, into the density of Parker's gut. She cracked her knuckles and headed back out to finish the show.

Jimmy's monthly bare-knuckle boxing tourneys always drew a bloated audience, like flies to a carcass. A little over a year ago, Parker had been one of those flies, fattening up on the decayed flesh of her past life, but slavering for something fresher. She spotted a poster for the fights at a single-tank gas-up off the state highway.

"Champion Boxing Tournament – One Night Only – $5 At Door, $4 Pitchers, $2 Hot dogs – Come Watch the Meanest Bastards of Hekla Lake Pulp Each Other Like Oranges – Jimmy's Gym, 1313 Main Street – Fighters Wanted."

After beating herself up across seventeen states to escape what she'd done, Parker couldn't easily pass up an opportunity to lay into a warmer body. On the twisting drive up the mountain to the village of Hekla Lake, high beams splashing across the tall grass and rocky canyon faces, Parker named her fists Shame and Loathing. That first night, she signed up and meted out her punishment to every man who took to the ring with her. But she was rusty, butt and back sore from too much driving, arms and legs weak from lifting no more than a gas nozzle and fill-up station burritos. She got laid out good and proper, but she put on enough of a show for Jimmy to invite her back the next month, and the month after that, and soon enough she was headlining. She earned a decent purse each match, more if she cleaned up the place for Jimmy after. Got herself a small room above the village's only pub, and hadn't quite worked up the sense required to blow out of town. But it wasn't the steady work that kept her around, or the hobo charm of the slack-jawed locals – she damn near hated everyone she met, when she couldn't avoid meeting them – or even the allure of sinking her knuckles into the ribs and jaws of a few cocky bastards every month. No, it was the hunts that kept Parker Eriksen in Hekla Lake.

The crowd of bloodthirsty locals and neighboring farmers and tradesmen boomed their ravenous joy through the small gym as Parker climbed back into the ring. It was a proper wrestling ring, set up in the center of the gym floor, all lifting and other training equipment swept to the sides of the place. Jimmy's Gym had probably once been a garage, all slab and draft, still harboring the faint and not unwelcome odor of gasoline and oil. Rows of folding chairs encircled the ring, each seat filled with the butt of a townie, of working folk looking to unwind with a spot of violence. Jimmy hired some high school kids from the valley to walk through the crowd, selling rollies and chew, priced-up cans of Coors and his own sister's lemon Jell-O shots. Jimmy himself tended the bar and ticket counter – a long white folding table where he pulled forties out of a cooler and emptied them into plastic pitchers. No one got ID'd at Jimmy's, and the booze and drugs flowed freely.

In her corner of the ring, Parker slumped against the ropes and sucked on her mouthguard. She endured pats on her bare shoulders from fans, offers of drinks and calls for blood. Her ears played tricks at the start of a bout, ghosted her with voices from her past. A gruff, "Keep that chin up," a chuckling, "Send him to hell, kid." Lately, her nose had been getting in on the game, wafting hints of a spearmint-and-grip powder bouquet she hadn't been in the presence of for years. She shook it all away, zeroed in on the opposite corner.

Her final opponent unbuttoned his flannel to puff his hairy chest for the cheers of the crowd, roaring through his beard, all but pulling out his dick to wave it around for praise. Parker didn't know this man – he wasn't one of Hekla's locals – but she knew what kind of fighter he was from his posturing alone. He matched her in height, but she overshadowed him in girth. He put work into his upper body but ignored his legs; he'd be slow, no foot work to speak of. He had a long reach, and he'd make her come to him. After he got a punch in – if he got a punch in – he'd gloat, do a little crowd work, leave his flank open for a counterstrike. She had him all figured out in the time it took his boner to press fully against the denim of his patchy jeans. Another flaw in his performance – the jeans, not the boner. Boners were typical for this kind of thing. No, the jeans, and the belt that secured them. Parker could use those to her advantage.

There was no dress code for the fighters, and few rules other than no kicking and no weapons in the ring. Parker always wore the same thing – tight-fitting sports bra and mid-thigh shorts, no shoes. She tied boxing tape across her knuckles and wrists, to lessen the risk of breaking her fingers or snapping her joints. Kept her fingernails short – a disadvantage since there was no rule against scratching, but she was more likely to bend and break them against someone's bone-hard muscles. She'd considered wearing a sweatband when she first started, but after watching a bout where one of the fighters choked out his opponent with his own band, she abandoned that idea. Besides, the sweat stinging her eyes sharpened her focus. Just because none of these yokels had the formal training she did, didn't mean they couldn't be ruthless. Jimmy's poster from a year ago had been truthful: these were some right mean bastards.

"Settle down, settle down," the referee called from the center of the ring. He was more emcee than ref, seeing as how he didn't do much but call KO when someone got knocked out, or tapped their surrender. His name was Johnson Holt, he was the cook at the Canyon Café, the only eatery in the village, aside from Patty's BBQ, which was more a cart than a proper diner. He was beefy and cheerful, a mountain man Santa Claus, all wild scruff and checkered flannel. Not young but not too old, typically smelled of balsam wood and pine. Parker only reluctantly knew how he smelled on account of he'd had to pull her off an opponent a time or two, when she got a little too focused, a little too sharp.

"All right now, ya'll," Johnson continued to shout. Despite the popularity of these tourneys, Jimmy refused to splurge on a mic or sound system. "Are you ready for the final bout of the night? The title bout of Jimmy's Gym's Champion Boxing Tournament? Let me hear ya!" When the noise quieted down, Johnson continued, "Our final contender enters the ring for the first time, to challenge your reigning champ, the Norse goddess made flesh herself: Hel!"

Johnson held an arm toward Parker. She raised her own arms in triumph and spun for the crowd. They ate it up, stamping and roaring and sloshing beer from their plastic cups. Outside the ring, many of these people didn't speak to Parker or know her real name. Folks in Hekla Lake tended to mind their own business, which suited Parker just fine. But her eye did alight on a handful of familiar faces, who cupped hands to sneering mouths and booed, or looked away from her entirely. Inside the ring, Parker was Hel, a Viking goddess of the battle-damned. Outside the ring, she was as much a pariah in her chosen small town as she'd been at the acme of her colossal mistakes in her old life. At least this time, it was on her terms, her choice, her hand-dug grave.

"And our fearless contender, ladies and assholes—" Riotous laughter at that jab, Johnson grinning at his own dull wit. "—hailing from Mill Valley, frothing at the mouth with rabid ferocity, his teeth itching to chip themselves on a goddess's divine bones – Lobo, the Wolf of the Valley!"

Lobo leapt onto the ropes and howled at the crowd, whose allegiances were as loose as the wads of cash they shoved at the teens plying them with pot and tobacco. The man bounced back into his corner, rocking up and down on the heels of his steel-toed boots. He wasn't frothing at the mouth exactly, but brown juice stained his chin from the crush of chew stuffed in his cheek.

"Will our champion and our contender please join me in the center of the ring?" Johnson called them forward.

They stood with the ref between them, sizing each other up. Lobo was jittery, pupils dilated and eyes burning with something more than adrenaline. His lips were chapped, his skin dry, dandruff even in his chest hair. Parker sneered around her mouthguard. She wasn't pretty, sure, but she was a damn sight cleaner than the Wolf of the Valley, and that made the Viking Goddess smugly proud. She was statue-still, a viper lying dormant in the grass, a silent volcano begging for eruption. Only her eyes moved as Johnson yelled out the official rules, meager as they were, and asked the fighters to touch knuckles before going back to their corners to await the bell.

Johnson fumbled himself over the ropes to stand on the outside of the ring. He held on with both hands, leaned back until his long hair nearly touched the knees of the front row of spectators, and shouted: "Fighters! Let the match…. BEGIN!"

At his ticket table bar, Jimmy slapped his palm down repeatedly on an old timey hotel bell. Lobo bounced a couple paces toward the center of the ring, diagonal from Parker's corner. She took up a half squat pose, and circled quickly to his left. His long legs strode right, as he laughed and howled, fists up in front of his gaping mouth. Parker aimed for his center of mass and scuttled forward, zigging right so he'd zag left, and then shifting weight to her outside leg and throwing a hook at his waist. He was too slow to block, and her stance was too short for him to land the wide counterpunch he threw at her head.

Parker resisted the old but insistent urge to drop a thigh kick right above his knee. Get him on the ground where she could make quick work of him. That wasn't how these boxing matches operated. Not enough spectacle on the ground. The matches didn't truck with points, either, so she followed up her hook with two quick jabs to the man's gut, while he was still recovering from his whiffed punch.

Lobo stepped back, arms now lowered to protect his middle, and spit tobacco sludge at Parker. The glob caught her on the neck. The crowd recoiled in disgust which quickly turned into undulating exuberance. They loved a good taunting. Lobo bared teeth the color of a week-old bruise at Parker. She turned away, slinking back into her corner to grab a towel, give Lobo an opportunity to come at her.

His heft buckled the floor of the ring as he bore down on her open rear. She spun at the last moment and easily ducked two wild jabs aimed, again, for her head. She came up hunched, connecting several quick blows to his ribs and armpits, before dodging an angry fist to twist around his back and meet him on his other side with another one-two to the waist. Lobo growled now, backed up to the ropes, and spat his frustration at her again. The globs fell short, splattering the mat.

In fights past, in her old life, Parker's next tact would be to dance Lobo away from the ropes. Get him back closer to center ring, confuse him with her short jabs, draw him after her so she could get behind him and wrap her legs around his neck for a takedown. But this wasn't fights past, or anything close to Parker's old life (thank Hel). She liked Lobo on the ropes good and fine; the crowd wanted a spectacle after all.

Parker hadn't been throwing hands at Lobo's waist just to befuddle him; with each landed hit, she worked her lightning-quick fingers against the tacky wolf's head belt buckle, strapped like a trophy above his crotch – where, Parker imagined, his boner was flaccidly fading. She straightened and strode with practiced speed toward Lobo. When she was close enough, Lobo's shoulder telegraphed his right hook. She dodged under his arm, punched his elbow into his gut, unhooked his loosened belt with her other hand, and slipped it free from his jeans. In the same fluid motion, she stepped up onto the ropes and threw her leg to the other side of Lobo, sitting on the top rope so her knees were level with his shoulders. She squeezed him in, looped the belt around his neck, and pulled. Tossing her head back, she let out a banshee call that the crowd drank in like a dime-store drunk tasting his first slug of top shelf bourbon.

Lobo grabbed Parker's wrists, trying to wrench her arms away. Bent back, struggling for breath, his feet couldn't find purchase. As he slipped and struggled, the referee dove under the ropes to enter the ring across from them, shouting to be heard over the crowd. Parker dropped the belt, and Lobo went tumbling after it. When he was on his knees, one hand to his neck, the other reaching out toward Johnson for some kind of assistance that he'd never get, Parker jumped back onto the mat and dealt one downward jab to Lobo's temple. His body slammed to the floor, wad of tobacco spitooning out of his mouth and onto Johnson's shiny black Timberlands.

Johnson lifted Lobo's head and gently peeled back his eyes to check his pupils, then held two fingers briefly to the fluttering pulse in Lobo's neck. Satisfied with the KO, Johnson let Lobo's head fall back down, unceremoniously kicked at the air until the tobacco wad dislodged from his own boot, and held his arms out toward Parker. "Your reigning champion!"

As was the custom, Parker walked the ring for her victory lap with arms held above her head. Johnson whirled in the center of the ring, jabbering accolades and reminding everyone that while Jimmy's was closing, the pub would be open for another three hours. Most of the crowd was happy, cheering and finishing up their smokes and cups, but some grumbled, annoyed that the match ended so quickly. Parker's matches usually ended quickly these days. She couldn't help it; she was getting bored.

If it wasn't for the hunts, she'd have left town by now. Probably. Maybe. Eh, who the fuck knew?

Jimmy approached her a month back, asked her to try to keep things interesting in the ring. Not throw the fights exactly, but maybe not try so hard. Go easy a little, put on more of a show. Parker agreed to get a little fancier – hence the belt move tonight – but not to give ground. Every bruise, gash, and broken bone on her person, Parker wanted to earn. To win. To pile like so much dirt into the places inside her left empty by the dynamite she'd thrown into the cavern of her old life.

Now, Parker ducked out of the ring and skirted the crowd on a beeline for the exit. She couldn't avoid Jimmy – she could never avoid Jimmy – because he was always working the door, and he had to count out her take, anyway.

"Not your best out there tonight," Jimmy said by way of greeting when she stepped up to his table. Wiry and balding, he wore crisp white tees and basketball shorts almost exclusively, even in winter. He might throw a parka over the tee, but the shorts were nonnegotiable. How else would he communicate to the exactly no one who cared that he was one hundred percent heterosexual?

"Crowd seemed to disagree," Parker said. She fought in damn near every match tonight, tried some new moves that got her knocked a couple times, and still pulled out a stunner of a chokehold in the title bout. Hell, she'd sacrificed another damn tooth on the altar of keeping things interesting in the ring. Jimmy could at least acknowledge that.

Jimmy sucked his teeth, counting out a stack of ones and fives from the cash box. "Eh, lots of chatter about the humdrum match ups. They can see it on your face, Eriksen, in your dragging moves. You're bored. And it's boring them."

Parker balled up the money Jimmy handed her, stuffed it into her bra. "Boring you?"

He thought it over, nodding at a few folks as the crowd made its way out of his gym in boisterous clusters. "Maybe. But I got some ideas for next month."

"Yeah?" Parker grabbed a pitcher of warming beer, chugged it hard. Jimmy shook his head but didn't look too peeved about it. She slammed it back onto the foldout, swiped her arm across her mouth. "Call my manager about those ideas. He'll set up a meeting."

Jimmy laughed. Parker's gut twisted. There was a time when that line wouldn't have been a joke. Parker dropped her mouthguard into the swill at the bottom of the pitcher, and elbowed her way out of the gym.

Hekla Lake was an old mining town turned doomed farm country. Its very name was a joke: the only "lake" to be found had, in day's gone, ran from the junction of three mountain-blown mines under the small valley paved to create the workers' village. It was a lake of fire that burned through barely usable ore and left only molten rocks and ash in its wake. The fire that burned out the mines essentially killed the village. It continued to survive only because land here was cheap, certain livestock did okay enough to get by, and tobacco could grow damn near anywhere.

There was one main road through the village – Main Street, natch – and four branching side streets. Main Street dead-ended into the mouth of a closed mountain-side mine. The west side of the village abutted a small national park, separated by a sea of tall grass sprouting from hard, nutrient-poor soil. Grazing animals and crops were kept to eastside homesteads. The village proper had exactly one of everything – grocery store, pub, gym, auto garage, hardware store, barber, mercantile. Looking for anything fancier, you had to drive down the winding road to Mill Valley, or even further for the nearest Walmart or another large box store. Other than the damn near illegal monthly boxing matches that drew a decent crowd to Hekla Lake, the only other type of visitors were hikers passing through to better camping in the national park, or looky-loos who'd caught the village's ten-minute segment on Haunted America and came to hunt ghosts. Parker figured the folks who ended up settling in Hekla Lake were trying to hide from their ghosts, not invite more over for tea.

Most of the locals heaped into two categories: Yuchi Natives or brawny mountain men, with a few long-suffering wives or listless widows thrown in as outliers. The Yuchi reclaimed the territory after the mining trade died its inevitable death, and its members were truly the only folks keeping the lights on in Hekla. They owned the shops and the land, and rented little farms to the mountain men. Parker herself took up in a studio above the pub, where she washed dishes and did other odd jobs to earn her keep. The money from the fights she shoved into a sock and packed away at the back of her closet, for who-knows-what some day. The hunts didn't earn her any dough. Those, she did for other reasons.

The pub was two blocks down from Jimmy's and across Main Street. Its lights blazed, hooting and hollering already wafting from the place like so much smoke. Patty was setting up her BBQ cart off to the side, a line already about ten deep, folks spilling over from Jimmy's, hands out for a plate. Parker stuck to the shadows of the road, shoulders hunched, trying to make it to her room unnoticed. Not easy, being tall and wide as she was, and still wearing her minimal fighting gear.

"Hey, Eriksen, hold up a minute."

This call hit Parker harder than any punch she'd taken in the ring tonight. She thought briefly about continuing on, pretending she hadn't heard, or all out running, even. But she thought better of it. In a town this small, it was best to face uncomfortable situations head-on. Hurtle through the discomfort, and nurse your wounds on the other side.

Parker turned. Sylvie Cahwee sprinted through the headlights of a muddy pickup, slapping her palm on the hood when the driver honked at her. This gesture was met with a gesture of the driver's own as he revved by. Sylvie wasn't wearing her park ranger uniform, so didn't command the same respect she might have otherwise. Her jeans were fashionably ripped, her oversized black fisherman's sweater maybe slightly too warm for the season. She slipped her unruly black hair into a rubber-banded ponytail as she planted herself in front of Parker. Her green eyes came to about Parker's chin, sparkling like gems against her skin, dark and smooth as a robin's belly. Parker had a hard time dragging her gaze away from noticing Sylvie's skin, remembering the last time she'd touched it.

"Where you off to so fast?" Sylvie asked.

Parker nodded her head toward the pub.

"Not to drink and be merry though, I'd wager?"

Parker quirked her lips in what passed as a smile, for her.

Sylvie ran a hand over the back of her neck, looking up and down the road, waving to a few people who made their way out of Jimmy's. Main Street had two street lamps, one at the crest of the hill that brought cars into town, and one at the closed-off mouth of the mountain to illuminate the orange-and-white signs warning cars away from the dead end. Most nights, the stars and moon, unfettered by city smog, shone bright enough to light the whole village without the aid of public electricity. It was the same tonight, although

Parker did notice patches of cotton white clouds rolling over a few nearby mountain peaks.

"Did you need something?" Parker didn't mean to sound terse, but it was kind of her default tone since burying herself in Hekla Lake. After her first match at Jimmy's, when she'd decided this was as good a place as any to languish in her guilt, Parker hammered walls up around herself like a tightly-nailed coffin. Only she hadn't been careful enough, not at first. She met Sylvie in the pub, got to talking and drinking, and it became a habit. Parker's booze-slicked tongue pried the nails loose from her coffin's lid and Sylvie peeked her goddamned beautiful head inside before Parker could close it back up.

About six months ago, the two stumbled up from the pub into Parker's studio, too drunk to make it to the bed, but not too drunk to undo each other's pants. The next morning, Parker withdrew, mortified. She considered leaving, tossing her meager possessions into her beater and puttering the hell out of town. She wasn't ashamed of what they'd done, but she was suddenly aware of just how much she'd let herself relax around Sylvie, just how much she'd let herself indulge in someone who didn't make her feel like shit. She didn't deserve that luxury, hadn't earned it yet, and probably never would. She balled up Shame and Loathing, knocked herself back to something resembling sense, and told Sylvie their night together had been a mistake.

While their socializing had stopped after that, Sylvie continued to be amiable with Parker, frustratingly friendly, sweet even. She waved when she saw Parker out and about, made chit chat if they were caught in line at the grocery store together, smiled at a jogging Parker if she passed her on the dirt road that led into the national park. Parker remained cold, her coffin airtight, but Sylvie's charm worked its way inside like a particularly stubborn worm.

"Shit, Eriksen, I just wanted to congratulate you on a good show. They got flyers for Hel all the way out to the airport now, you know." Sylvie raised her fingers toward Parker's face. Parker flinched. Sylvie lowered her arm, tsking. "Can't believe you let Connor pop you one, though. You might need stitches above that eye."

Parker touched her brow, sucking in a wince. Connor Allen was a mechanic at the garage. Young, stupid and ugly, but fast and with a wild fighting style Parker couldn't quite get a bead on. He got in a few good slaps early in the evening's bouts, but when she finally caught his squirrelly ass, she made him regret it. He'd also loosened the tooth she'd had to spit out into the sink before the final match with Lobo.

"It'll heal fine," Parker said, dropping her hand back to her side. The silence between them was heavier than the artery-clogging sauce Patty slathered on her signature beef ribs. Parker should have just shrugged and walked away, but some deeply ingrained sense of cordiality kept her rooted to the spot.

"Well, listen," Sylvie rocked back on her heels, stuffed her hands in the butt pockets of her jeans. "I don't know if you heard, but a freak snowstorm is headed this way. Supposed to hit the valley by morning. So, Bud and some of the others are pushing up the hunt. I just thought you'd want to know."

Parker's blood, chilled out after leaving the ring, flushed hot again. "Pushing it up to when?"

"Midnight, of course," Sylvie tsked again. "You know Bud and his dramatics. Anyway, have a good night, Eriksen. Be careful out there." Sylvie broke away from Parker, following the last of Jimmy's patrons down the street and disappearing into the pub.

Parker followed the side street that led out to some of the homesteads, and circled around to the back of the pub, her blood thrumming. A couple of groups stood around smoking in the yard, but they were easily sidestepped. Parker keyed her way in the back door, took the narrow wooden stairs up to the second floor three at a time, and let herself into her apartment with shaking hands.

She hadn't heard about the snowstorm – it didn't feel cold enough for that, and was extremely early in the season besides – but if it meant pushing up the hunt, she very much welcomed it. She was excited now, sweating out the whiskey she'd downed during the lackluster fights, shaking off the awkwardness of having got the news from Sylvie in the first place. Her night wasn't going to end how it normally did – hunkered in her secondhand recliner, cradling a tallboy in one hand and her dog in the other, trying to watch trashy reality TV through unfocused eyes as the spotty satellite blinked in and out. Tonight, she was going to earn some small sliver of her Sisyphean redemption. Tonight, Parker Eriksen was going to hunt down her demons made flesh – and beat them to death.

Chapter Two

At seven to midnight, Parker crouched low in the tall grass of the valley that separated Hekla Lake from the edge of the national park. From her position, she saw the rising curve of Mount Shafah, dark fir trees crawling over it like ants. On the other side of this mountain, the trees sloped into a canyon, skipped a dry creek bed that dripped with water following rainstorms, and then rose again across a series of hills, sliced through by worn hiking trails making up the bulk of the park. That was what the hunt was protecting: the park, its native fauna and flora, its attraction for tourists, its very integrity.

Considering this, it was odd to Parker that Sylvie had never participated in a hunt. Sure, she helped coordinate on occasion – or, like tonight, passed a tip on to Parker, who wasn't officially participating herself – but certainly not in the official capacity for which her being a ranger could easily allow. As far as Parker knew, the hunts were sanctioned and funded by the government. In order to legally take part, you had to register online, submit to a background check, account for every bullet released and every kill marked. Parker preferred to skip all of that. Some of the things she'd fled would surely track her down if she entered her vital statistics into a government database.

Fortunately, early in her career at Jimmy's, she'd impressed a woman from California, passing through on an RV tour of the 'States, by roundly breaking her jaw in the ring. Her name was Katja, she said, a Bulgarian of ancestry but a Canadian of birth and now an American by naturalization, having, unfortunately, fallen in love with an American and married him, much to her parent's disapproval. Parker learned all of this, and more, holding Katja's hand as her neck lolled on the mat, while waiting for the ambulance. It wasn't the first time Parker had broken someone's jaw in the course of her work, but it was the first time that person remained quite so chatty following the incident.

"My husband—he's drinking over at the pub, can someone get him? Cell service is shit in this canyon. Shit! He always has to have a drink and play a couple'a hands of poker over there when we pass through Hekla. His buddy tends bar there. Grew up together, they did, somewhere even middler of nowhere than this. What's that sound? D'ya hear that? Clack... clack... clacking?"

That sound was her own teeth rattling around in her splintered bones. Her speech was slurred but steady, continuous, pain no doubt kept at bay due to the shock of her concussion. Parker tried to get her to shut up, but also had to keep her awake, and she sure as hell wasn't going to be the one doing the talking. She yelled for someone to collect Katja's husband, gave her hand a squeeze to ensure the woman could squeeze back, then focused the woman's roving eyeballs back to her face by snapping her fingers in front of her nose.

"What was I saying? My husband's buddy, yeah, he's always trying to get us to do local things, get involved, like the pie eating contest in July, or the snowmobile race in January. Or this, ha ha, these boxing things. I don't box but I lift, do you lift? I can deadlift two-fifty with my back belt. Just a hobby. I'm strong, right? I showed you that, at least."

She wasn't lying. She'd broken through Parker's defenses a time or two during the match, bruised up her cheek and reddened her ear, may have even fractured a rib if the pain in Parker's side was any indication. The sirens of the ambulance, inching its way up the mountain from Mill Valley, sang a hallelujah chorus in Parker's uninjured ear.

"Never would'a jumped in this ring, ha ha, but for you, you cunt. Ha! A woman on the bill, the champion, no less. I had to see that. Take my chances. Test my mettle. You understand? You understand. We have to prove ourselves. Against each other, right? What does it mean we can best a man? Nothing! Ha!"

Katja spit blood and teeth onto her chest. A commotion rattled amorphously beyond Parker's field of vision; folks clearing a path for the approaching EMS workers.

"Men are weak, yeah? We love them like puppies. Like delicate flowers. Who cares you can punch out a man? Who can't do that? A puppy, maybe. A flower can't. So, I thought, yes, I have to try this woman, put my two hundred-and-fifty-pound biceps against whatever the hell she's got. Ha ha but you got something, don't ya? Tricks. Secrets. Ways. Oh, who's touching me? What's happening? Hey, hey!"

The EMS workers not so delicately moved Parker aside as they surrounded Katja, dodging her flailing arms and her tumbling words as they slid the stretcher under her and tried to snap on a neck brace. Katja's eyes focused on Parker's over the shoulder of one of the workers. Truly focused, so sharp it stopped Parker dead as she was lifting a rope to escape.

"Man and woman, you can best, easy, right, cunt? Champion Cunt? Too easy. Means nothing. What about a beast, eh, champ? Pit your mettle against tusks, then come tell me who is strongest? Ask my husband, ask his buddy, what—hey! That pinches! Stop spinning me—don't spin me!"

The EMS workers carried Katja out of the ring, past the press of looky-loos, out of the gym, the only thing spinning were her eyes in her skull, trying to match the running of her mouth.

Parker didn't think much of the woman's ramblings at the time; she had two more opponents to fight that night, and was meeting Sylvie after for a drink. But, lying in bed later, listening to the rhythm of her dog's snores, trying not to flash on images of Sylvie's neck as she gulped hard cider, her eyelashes as she blinked away tears from laughing so hard at one of Parker's anecdotes, her fingers as they threatened to alight upon Parker's own, white-knuckling her beer stein to keep from shaking. Then, Parker's thoughts ran for cover behind Katja's words. She was right, after all. Beating these untrained men was easy, no matter how beefy, how much weight they could press, deadlift or curl. Brute strength was nothing when Parker, who'd built up her own brute strength over the years, also had technique, strategy, cunning. Rage probably also helped; guilt-fueled and redemption-seeking. What man could stand against that? What woman? None in Hekla had, at least so far.

What had that woman said, then, about a beast? Could she, Parker, Champion Cunt (she thought she could make some money stitching that onto t-shirts, let Jimmy sell them for a 60-40 split at the matches. That would spotlight Parker more than she already was, draw crowds from further and further afield, her reach stretching perhaps far enough back the way she'd come to inadvertently grasp the attention of someone from her past. No, Parker had let her greed, her entrepreneurial spirit, a particular individual had called it at one point, get the best of her before, and she would not let that happen again—couldn't let it happen again.) Could Parker Eriksen best a beast in a fight? A tusked beast, presumably with no weapons other than her fists? Would years of training, crafting her skill, learning how to read her opponents' bodies, would any of that mean anything as she stared down such a creature?

The next morning, Parker caught one of the bartenders as he was unloading a truck of canned beer and bagged pretzels. She helped him lift a few crates, then asked about any good hunting in the area. She wasn't even sure if he was Katja's husband's buddy; she had a fifty-fifty chance. It was him or the owner, who had rented her the room and let her do small jobs around the building and grounds to keep it, and was not now, nor ever could have been, described as anyone's "buddy."

Cob Kulla was older than salt, with hair the same color, and a build similarly crusty. He came by weekly to check on things, collect rent, complain about his back, and marvel at the historical magnificence of a tribal-owned town whose success couldn't be claimed by white man's government.

"Game's fair if you get out past the canyon," the bartender was saying. He hefted another crate of beer and shuffled through the pub's basement entrance, Parker holding the door for him. "Small game, though. Rabbits, badgers, birds. The big stuff's protected, mostly holes up in the park, your elks and your moose. They got seasons for the bigger stuff, though. Population control, you know. I'm not much of a hunter myself. You should ask your friend, the ranger, about it."

Parker didn't like the tilt of the bartender's knobby head or the gleam in his brown eyes as he referenced her "friend."

"What about animals with tusks?" She asked, taking the crate he'd carried and heaving it onto the stack she'd already brought in. "I was told there were some beasts with tusks around these parts needed killing."

The bartender pulled a stained rag from his back pocket, removed his ball cap, and swiped sweat from his forehead. "Who told you that?"

"Buddy of yours. Fought his wife in the ring last night. Katja?"

"No shit?" He huffed a laugh, looked askance at the basement ceiling, shook his head a little. "That Katja talks too damn much. Well, yeah, there's 'tusk hunting,' as you say, but it ain't very sporting, if you ask me."

That's when Parker learned about the glut of feral hogs blighting the national park, and surrounding farming towns.

She didn't get all of it from the bartender that day. She ended up talking to Jimmy, and the infamous Patty of Patty's BBQ, before finally broaching the topic with Sylvie, despite her trepidation after the way the bartender had said her name.

"Why are you asking me about feral hogs?" The ranger questioned around a mouth full of peanuts. They sat across from each other in a pub booth, Sylvie coming off a shift and Parker having a beer or two in preparation for a night of washing dishes. "Ever heard of Google?"

Parker's knee bumped into Sylvie's under the table. "I skimmed half a Wikipedia page before I gave up."

Hekla didn't truck much with wi-fi, on account of being mostly built into the side of a canyon, but all the required hardware for wired internet and cable TV alike had been installed throughout town just a couple years ago. Reception on both, just as it was on cell phone reception, was spotty at best.

"Ugh, they're like cockroaches," Sylvie said. Her finger grazed Parker's as she plucked more peanuts out of the bowl in front of her. Parker struggled to pay attention to the ranger's words, and not the heat rising up from her groin at the touch. "Some dipshit brought wild boars over from Europe, those mated with domesticated sows, and voila—invasive species. They breed like mad, travel in large families, eat basically anything, and have no natural predators."

Parker sipped her tall boy. "Are they huge?"

"Nah, not like a farm pig. But they're all muscle, a bit like someone I know." The dim light in the pub masked Parker's blush. "And they're aggressive, extremely territorial, and they smell awful. That part's not like you, you regularly smell good."

"Any around here?" Parker asked before she could dwell on that remark.

"Some, but the state has a program to keep their numbers down. The thing is, Eriksen, they aren't good for shit. Actually, their shit might be the only useful thing they produce, if you turned it into fertilizer."

"What's so bad about them?"

Sylvie counted off on her salty fingers. "One, they're riddled with disease. Wouldn't be surprised to find ticks carrying bubonic plague glutting out on their hides. So you can't eat 'em. Two, their fur and their hides are too coarse and nasty to bother making into pants or something. It wouldn't be worth the cost. Same goes for their tusks, there's no money in that ivory. For three, did I mention their smell? Like a skunk mated with a rotten egg and gave birth to sulfuric skunk-egg babies."

Parker laughed at Sylvie's shiver of disgust. "All right, so we've got giant smelly cockroaches who eat everything. Why haven't I seen these ugly dudes yet?"

"Because of the hunts." Sylvie explained through pauses to sip beer, steal Parker's peanuts, and press her knee harder against Parker's, that most states had their own tax-funded eradication programs for their feral hog problem. The official hunt in these parts ran all year round depending on need, was conducted by a local elected leader, and was staffed by registered hunters who were each outfitted with automatic rifles larger than the hogs themselves. Most of these hunters chased down packs of hogs in their Jeeps and Chevys, with spotlights and infrared and night vision goggles to boot. "Hell," Sylvie said, "Natalie Palmer, that gal who owns Mill Valley's local news station? She rents out their traffic helicopter for the hunts. Pilots it herself most of the time, while these camo-clad Army rejects hang out the side and pump thousands of rounds into anything vaguely hog shaped."

Parker's skull was thick, but not dense enough to miss the ranger's clear disdain. "You disagree with this method?"

"It's coward shit, Eriksen. It's not sportsmanlike, it's not even civil. These guys act like they're doing this to protect our land, but that's bullshit. They're doing it to stoke their own egos, so they can jizz to the memories later when their wives won't fuck them because they smell like—"

"—sulfuric skunk egg babies," Parker finished for her.

After their laughter ebbed, Sylvie elaborated. It was the national park that these hunting crews fancied themselves as saving. The farming crops and cattle, being situated at the other side of the canyon, with the Village of Hekla Lake between them, were plenty sheltered from wild animal attack, even of the feral hog variety. In fact, farmers had more to fear from insects ruining their livelihoods – and the pesticides used to curtail those insects – than from feral hogs. But that was true about the threat feral hogs posed to most species, Sylvie mused, despite the destruction they undoubtedly caused to ecosystems over time. Owing to several attacks on high profile humans, and the subsequent overblown media coverage of same, feral hogs had become to rural farmers, landowners, and country dwellers what sharks had become to beachgoers, pleasure boat owners, and ocean swimmers: vicious monsters poised to attack any human who dared wander into their domain.

"Feral hogs attack maybe five people annually," Sylvie said. "Cows kill more people than feral hogs or sharks combined. Fucking cows."

By this time, both women had put away a beer too many, and were giggling through their discourse. Parker had to get back into the kitchen, and Sylvie had to sober up enough to drive home to Mill Valley, so they wrapped things up. Sylvie gave Parker the number of someone to call if she had more questions, blew her a friendly kiss, and slid out of the booth. Tying on her apron, Parker stolidly avoided lingering on that goodbye by ruminating on what she'd learned. She had no qualms about keeping the hog population at bay, but she did agree the lengths to which the general public had collectively decided to go in order to achieve this mission – the automatic weapons, army-grade technology, armored vehicles – was not only cowardly, as Sylvie lamented, but entirely devoid of humanity.

If you couldn't take down your enemy humanely, did you deserve to take him down at all?

Fortunately, thanks to Sylvie, Parker was able to negotiate herself into the hunt without abiding by all the red tape. Even now, after everyone knew about the dissolution of that friendship, they allowed her to continue to join in the hunt on the fringes, probably for the sheer spectacle of it. Parker could feel the eyes of the villagers, up in their safe, warm bedrooms, searching for her dark shape out in the valley. She was thankful for the spotty internet, the unreliable cellular service; otherwise, she might find herself going viral across more than just the curious minds of the locals and the hunters.

Seven minutes until midnight. Six, now. Parker felt the wind change, and hunkered lower.

It had gotten colder by degrees since she'd left Jimmy's. The clouds amassed thickly, blotting out the stars, obscuring the bulk of the opalescent moon. The wind kicked up, whirling haphazardly through town, causing folks to lower windows and close shutters. On her walk to the valley, Parker encountered several swirls of what could have been snowflakes, if not ash from coal fireplaces being lit throughout town. A cold front was on its way, was here already, in fact, but Parker remained skeptical about an all-out snowstorm.

In any case, despite the mounting cold, Parker wore what she always wore for the hunt: a pair of midthigh black Lycra shorts, a dark moisture-wicking tank top, water shoes with rubber soles that were form-fitted around each individual toe, and her knuckles and wrists wrapped in boxer's tape. Over this, she wore a bright yellow reflective vest, with strips of the same material stitched into the seams of her shorts, and taped along her forearms. Unlike in the ring, Parker did wear a sweatband out on the hunts, reflective and yellow. This was for the benefit of the other hunters, so they didn't accidentally shoot her if they followed the feral hogs into her kill zone. The hogs, the Internet told her, didn't see in color, and were nearly blind in the dark.

Usually, Parker didn't join the hunts at night, on account of the disadvantage it gave the hogs. But she didn't want to risk missing her chance at any hunt at all for days to weeks to even months if a snowstorm really did come through.

Five minutes to midnight. Parker cracked her knuckles, rolled her neck, flexed her toes. She smelled pine and shit and grass and unfallen snow. Distantly, she thought she heard the rotors of a helicopter whirring to life.

Unbidden, Parker's mind flashed onto thoughts of Sylvie. Specifically, Sylvie at one of the windows behind her, her eyes goring into Parker's back sharper than any feral hog's tusk. The idea was ridiculous; Sylvie didn't live in the village, or take up with anyone who did. At least, not as far as Parker knew, which wasn't very far, she realized. Maybe Sylvie did take up with someone in the village. Maybe she was too busy taking up with someone at this very moment to care to look out of the fogged-up bedroom window to see Parker, crouching like an idiot in the grass, clenching her fists like some kind of lifeline.

Four minutes. Enough. Parker shook her head. The wind picked up. The horizon out beyond the mountain glowed brighter. The helicopter chopped through the sky much clearer now. Three minutes. Two. She held her breath.

All at once, the hogs burst from the tree line. Snorts and huffs, screeching and snarling. Their hooves beat a terrified path from the cover of the trees as the helicopter whooshed over top of them, its blades whirling, bullets popping off, chasing the hogs into the open ground of the valley. The wind from the helicopter's blades laid the grass low, revealing Parker's position. The spotlight from the helicopter blinded her for a moment, and she gave a little annoyed wave. Then the chopper tilted, spun back toward the forest, and left her in darkness once more.

The feral hogs ran in a confused tangle through the valley, pivoting and barking their frustration as the helicopter corralled them. As one neared her, Parker let out her breath. Her lungs released her battle cry, and she leaped.

She had the hog by the tusks before it knew what hit it. She pulled its face down and shoved its muzzle into the dirt, disorienting it. Unlike inside Jimmy's ring, here there were no rules. Parker could use her feet, her elbows, her knees. Hell, she could even bite the damn beast if she wished. It certainly wouldn't balk at the chance to bite her. She kneed the hog in the flank, still holding it by the tusks, pinning it to the ground. It rolled, thrashing, and she dodged its flailing hooves to straddle it. She let go of one tusk and cocked back her arm, raining down blow after blow with her left fist – Shame – onto its snotty snout.

When the hog stopped moving, she dropped its second tusk, letting its head pound back into the dirt. She moved away from this one as the helicopter made another pass, illuminating the field of flesh-and-blood whirling dervishes. Parker locked onto her next target, and ran toward it.

A hog knocked into her knees mid-stride, sending her sprawling. It trampled her shins and took a toothy swipe at her forearm as she twisted around to palm-strike its snout. Stunned, the beast stumbled back. Parker headbutted it right above the eyes, causing stars to burst in front of her. She kicked the hog in the belly, laying it out, and kicked and kicked and kicked until its hard flesh caved in like a Jack O'Lantern three weeks after Halloween.

Parker clapped dirt off her hands, shook the viscera off her shoe, and launched herself at another hog.

It went on like this. Parker lost herself in it, gave herself over to the moment, the series of moments. She left her mind and fully entered her body. Nothing in the world existed except her flesh, blood, and bones, in direct opposition to that of the feral hogs. She felt every sinew in her arms grow taut as she poised to punch another viscous snout. Her own pheromones wafted violently out of every pore as she wrapped her legs around the coarse neck of a hog and jerked, snapping its spine. Gooseflesh sprouted along her skin in fevered beads, sweat soaked through her headband, turning it into little more than a soggy lasagna noodle. She punched, she kicked, she jumped, elbowed, kneed, tackled, and headbutted. Her breath beat through her in time with the flushed throbbing of her heart. She never felt more alive than she did during these hunts. More attuned to herself, and to her suffering.

And oh, did she suffer. More often than not, her fists caught more tusk than snout, scraping flesh off her knuckles despite the boxing tape. Her legs got beat to shit, battered by tusks, hard heads, hooves, and ramming bodies. Her shoulders and biceps took a bite or two, her forearms essentially one big bruise as she blocked counterstrike after counterstrike. Sweat, blood, mucus and marrow caked her nostrils, her ears, crusted her lips and eyes. She didn't even want to begin to imagine what was lodged under her fingernails. She was sore, aching, uncomfortable, disgusting and disgusted. She barfed when a hog ran full tilt into her stomach, then punched Loathing down into that barf to beat the beast into the ground. She was splattered with so much gunk her reflective vest and strips were all but useless. No matter. The hunt was nearing its end.

In a good hunt, Parker beat her way through thirty to fifty feral hogs before the fatigue swept in like a plague. There were fewer hogs tonight, though, probably owing to the oncoming storm, the later hour, the irregularly early season, or some combination of these. In any case, she was barely winded after working over just thirteen hogs when the helicopter's whipping blades receded, taking the light with it. The hogs scurried back into the forest, skirting by her with only a snort or a wheeze of acknowledgement. She had time to notice the wind had sharpened, the air crisp and brittle as an icicle, and to stick out her tongue and catch a few snowflakes before locking eyes with two feral yellow orbs through the grass.

It had been stalking her. Sizing her up. Biding its time. Its brethren rushed past it left and right and it didn't even twitch. Parker stood deathly still, half-turned toward the beast, readying for its attack. It inched slowly toward her, hooves barely making a sound as it scuffed along the mud. Snow fell, catching in the spiky brown fur of its ears and face. It was almost beautiful.

Something exploded in the forest. Parker instinctively looked toward the sound, taking her eyes off the beast. A column of dark black smoke and sparking embers plumed between the trees near the top of the mountain, lighting the sky on fire. An f-bomb tumbled out of her blood-stained mouth less than a second before the feral hog slammed into her.

She caught its tusks as her head slammed into the mud. She blinked away the urge to close her eyes. The thing's slobbering face was inches from hers, its breath hot and thick, tongue protruding past blackened teeth. Those yellow eyes never left hers as it scrambled for purchase, tugging its head from side to side, trying to shake her hands off its tusks so it could get to the soft flesh of her neck.

Parker planted her knees into the grooves of the thing's waist, just above the groin, to keep its hind legs from pummeling her kidneys. Its front hooves used her shoulders as a Stairmaster, but she couldn't block the blows without releasing the much more dangerous tusks. She attempted a headbutt, cutting her forehead on its gnashing teeth. She tried to roll it over, get on top of it, find her advantage, but it was much larger than the others she'd faced tonight, by at least a hundred pounds. Katja may have been able to bench its bulk, but Parker couldn't hope to. She was stuck.

The feral hog belched into Parker's nose, causing her to gag. It bucked and squirmed, digging its hooves into her collarbone. Something snapped, and Parker cried out. The hog screamed back at her. "Fuck you!" Parker screamed into the hog's gaping maw. "Fuck you!"

There was nothing for it: Parker had to leave the sanctity of her body and throw herself back into her mind, back into her past. She had to retrieve the training she'd steadfastly buried in the coffin one gravestone over from hers when she holed up here in Hekla Lake. It was time to bust out her Brazilian mixed martial arts basic ground defense technique.

Falling back into her training as an MMA fighter would have been as sweet and whimsical as riding a bike, except for all the bad memories that invariably accompanied it. She was thankful for the rules of Jimmy's fights, which limited her access to these memories by prohibiting most of the moves her training in Brazilian jiujitsu had instilled. As Parker assessed that the hog basically had her in guard position on the ground, she flashed on to a memory of her former coach taking her slow-motion through how to break the guard on her very first day of training. She had been so young, so naively full of herself. She'd barely paid attention. Her manager always told her she was a natural talent, creative, had her own style, did things her way, and won. She always won, until she didn't.

The feral hog's hoof struck her arm, bringing her back to its slavering mouth. As much as it repulsed her, the only way to break the thing's guard was to pull it closer. Parker sucked in a breath, tensed her abs, and twisted the hog's head to the side. She pulled it close, bending her neck so her temple pushed against the beast's flea-bitten ear. She kept their heads pressed together as she released its left tusk and shoved her forearm, palm flat, under its chin, and heaved her whole body against it. When she'd created enough space between its undercarriage and her stomach, she swept her leg sideways and brought herself into a crouch. Then she pivoted the arm that was under its chin, swung her body wide, and she was on top of the animal now, riding its bewildered back as it bucked against her chokehold.

"Hah!" She cried. "Hah hah, motherfucker!" She pounded Loathing into the side of its head until its legs buckled and it stopped moving beneath her. "Natural talent this, you sonofabitch!" She struck and struck and struck, until the hog's yellow eyes dimmed and glossed over, and its face was nothing but pulp.

Parker sat astride its back, grasped its neck as if she were holding onto a horse's reins, arched back, threw her chin to the sky, and howled. The wind ripped her triumph away, sending snow and ash down her throat. Suddenly, her body felt leaden, overcome with exhaustion. She fell sideways off the hog, into a soft mound of snow that had only minutes ago been grass. She laughed, and cried, and, quicker than she should have, Parker fell asleep.

Chapter Three

F ifteen years ago, if Parker Eriksen, Viking Queen of the Underworld, Champion Cunt, was the goddess of anything, it was of failure. Born into immense wealth in Trondheim, victory in life was all but assured, to be won either through merit or bought with money. Her father was a powerful magnate in the trade world, a business Parker knew precious little about, and couldn't give two shits to learn. All she really knew was he travelled all around the globe, sometimes bringing Parker with him on his excursions, where she complained about being trapped in a series of luxurious hotels, penthouses, yachts and vacation homes, while simultaneously texting all her friends to make them jealous. Her mother was some sort of royalty, a descendent of one ancient Norwegian queen or another (perhaps even a Viking queen?), whose inherited wealth could rival that of infamous magical orphan Harry Potter. Parker wanted for nothing, and wanted everything, until she got it, then she wanted nothing and no one and threw a tantrum until someone who had money spent it on her in a way she wouldn't know would please her until it either did or it didn't, and the cycle renewed itself.

In short, Parker Eriksen was a spoiled brat.

Unlike her three older brothers, she possessed neither charm, wunderkind intelligence, nor beauty. Mason, the eldest by a decade, was as handsome as a gourd, but possessed a business acumen their father regularly praised and employed. The twins, Virgil and Samson, seven years Parker's senior, volleyed genetic traits back and forth seemingly at their whimsy. If Virgil, the be-freckled redhead, was making headlines for dropping a scathingly sarcastic witticism on social media, then Samson, the chiseled blonde, was garnering front-page news in the entertainment section for what he wore to one industry awards show or another. Next weekend, they'd swap: Samson the droll academic, Virgil the vapid model, and around skipped the merry-go until Parker vomited.

Meanwhile, here was Parker sobbing into her champagne, alone and lonely in a hot bubble bath the size of an indoor pool, where even the jets couldn't distract her from her singular misery. She was sixteen, and should have been at school, but she regularly skipped out after third or fourth period. This led to her first failure – second, if you count the genetic one, which Parker certainly did – that of failing so many classes that she was kicked off of the lacrosse team where she served only to warm the diamond-encrusted benches donated by her family's estate last season. Thanks to her father's generosity, she was a senior at an American prep school, and would not, at this rate, graduate. Even her father, to whom Parker was currently texting wildly elaborate streams of crying emojis, couldn't buy her way into a diploma. It was a slow news week for invasive media, so they sprang on the story of the youngest Eriksen scion's imminent blunder like trapdoor spiders all vying for the same measly scrap of horsefly. Her father was too busy to care, Mason heeled at his side like a good doggy, and the twins were on some sort of holiday in a country that evidently didn't have wi-fi. Her mother was similarly lying low, taking her annual off-grid solo retreat from the stresses of parenting three adult children and one teenager, none of whom lived with her and all of whom had their own full-time staff.

It was her parents' fault, Parker mostly believed. After all, they were the ones who had her so late into their childbearing years that they were mainly bored by her, when they weren't outrightly annoyed or exhausted. She was raised by a series of au pairs, none of whom paid her much parental attention, and one of whom, when she was thirteen and ran full tilt into puberty, paid her too much attention (her father fired him before he could do too much damage, or so he hoped, and greased so many palms to keep the incident out of the news that he was starting to feel like a fry cook at an all-night diner). Truth be told, Parker counted that young man as her first true love, and hated her father for sending him away, and hated herself even more for wanting – craving – the attention he had bestowed upon her and which, he assured her from the beginning, no other man would ever want to gift her.

So, it wasn't really her fault, Parker surmised, when her parents sent her away to this American school, and set her up in this lavish three-story apartment with a staff she got to boss around between homework assignments, that she didn't exactly thrive academically. That she did, instead, fall into a depression so deep it looked, from the outside, like wallowing in her wealth and privilege, and was, on the whole, incredibly irritating. She was fair game to the media, owing to the fact that she was so awful, and the rest of her family, by contrast, so amazing; the Eriksens could afford to be taken down a peg or two, even (or especially) if it was Parker they had to shove off the ladder.

In the bath, Parker blocked her father's number, threw her cell phone across the tiles, and dunked her head under the bubbles. She thought about staying there forever. It was warm, and quiet, and it probably smelled pretty nice if she was fool enough to inhale. Maybe she should inhale. Open her mouth wide and gulp deep. One final red mark against her father's reputation, a dark blemish on her brothers' perfect shining complexions, to follow them around for the rest of their perfect lives. Only, her suicide would probably end up helping them all; unending sympathy falling like glitter on their mourning shoulders. Offer after offer of book and movie deals. Her death painted as a tragedy for them all, when really they'd forget her name in a matter of weeks following the funeral. Did her mother even know her name now? When was the last time she'd spoken with her mother? Last Christmas, or the Christmas before that?

Parker resurfaced, got out of the tub, and toweled off. She picked her phone up off the floor and sent video chats to her friends back in Scandinavia. Did they even know her name? Everyone called her Two, or Twosies, because there was already another Parker in the friend group when she'd elbowed her way in. She didn't want to go by her middle name, because it was her mother's name, and at this point, when they bothered to introduce her around at parties or other functions, her friends automatically called her Twosie Eriksen, as if that were and had always been her legal name. Well, fuck them. Fuck them! Parker shouted at the crystal-framed bathroom mirror. Fuck all of them!

After she got dressed and had one of the staff prepare her a ham and cheese sandwich for lunch, Parker left the apartment to go pretty much anywhere but school. Her email inbox was already overflowing with unread messages from the administration, her teachers, teammates the Lacrosse coach roped in to pretending to care about her. She was determined not to give a fuck – today, at least – about them, or her family, or anyone, and especially not about the person she saw when she passed by a floor-to-ceiling display window of high fashion and caught her own sallow reflection staring back. Sunken eyes in a too-pale face, moles that were too hairy to be termed beauty marks pocking a too-wide jaw, a too-large nose, and a thoroughly unimpressive forehead. Her hair was okay, but it was plain, a dull black that looked like a once-dark t-shirt that had gone through the wash more than enough times. She was too fat, and too tall, and had no fashion sense, and goddammit, fuck her. Fuck her, too.

Parker wouldn't have looked twice at the concrete gym that spread out for a whole city block along the alley she turned down to avoid any more shop windows, if it hadn't been for the flock of pigeons that flew overhead just as she stepped off the curb into the shadow of the building. She looked up at their coos as they swooshed past, and received a glob of bird poop in her eye for her curiosity. Cursing, flapping about, she stumbled down the alley, resisting the urge to scream for help or to get out her phone and call her driver to come get her. She bumped into someone hard, who caught her arm, and swiped a towel across her face.

"Hang on there, ick, I think I got it." When Parker could see again, she saw a woman taller than her, almost as wide, with muscles so sharp they pierced her tank top like knives. Sweat glistened on her black skin, everything rippling as she moved the towel delicately across Parker's awestruck face. Her touch was far softer than her physique would suggest. She tsked, pressed fingers beneath Parker's chin to tilt her head up, appraised her work.

"That bird got you good, kid." Her lips smacked around a glob of gum, spearmint knuckling up against the odor of fresh bird shit. "You want to come in and wash your face?"

Parker looked at the woman dumbly for more seconds than was normal, finally found her voice. "Y-yes. Thank you. Yes."

Inside, the gym was one gigantic open space, sectioned off only by different types of equipment, four square boxing rings marking each quadrant. Two men sparred in the ring furthest from the locker room toward which the woman led Parker. She stared as, in the span of an unblinking eye, they went from pummeling each other in a flurry of fists and grunts, to hugging each other, laughing, kissing the tops of each other's heads through their spitty mouthguards. She felt herself grinning, some new emotion welling up in her chest. She turned away, following the woman into the locker room.

This room smelled a lot worse than the gym proper – sweat, rubber, chalk and bleach that engulfed Parker like a bearhug – but was just as spacious, and clean, if untidy. Towels and clothes, open duffel bags, a variety of gear, cluttered the red-painted benches. The shiny black lockers that lined the walls were mostly hanging open, empty or revealing magazine pinups taped to their innards, sticks of deodorant and used sweatbands spilling out. The woman stopped at a double-wide entryway, beyond which Parker could see a black tiled floor and a row of stainless-steel stalls.

"Here you go." The woman waved Parker through. "Take your time with that, okay? But, heads up, this here's a unisex bathroom, so don't gasp too hard if one of the guys comes in to take a piss, all right? You'd be inflating their egos, and lord knows none of them is hurting for that."

The woman left Parker to it. She set her purse down on the sprawling, red-trimmed sink counter. Before she even looked in the mirror, she ducked her head under the hot water faucet and combed out the worst of the bird's poop. She had to remove several barrettes, which she chucked in the trash, not wanting any sort of remembrance of the incident. Her hair thoroughly flushed, she lifted one eyelid to peek in the mirror, assessing the damage to her face. Her temple and left cheek were smeared with whitish brown goop, edging into her nostril and streaking dangerously close to her upper lip. With an anguished cry, Parker stuck her face back under the faucet and scrubbed with her fingernails until her face looked like a cat had really worked her over.

Parker let the redness ebb a little and blow-dried her hair with the hand dryer. Her shirt was ruined, her make-up – caked on with no real strategy to begin with – clung to her face in splotches she didn't care to even out. All she wanted was to get back to her apartment, draw the curtains in her bedroom, bury herself in a nest of sweatpants and blankets, and maybe force one of the staff to watch a movie with her.

Back out in the gym, Parker found the woman who'd helped her crouched next to a man doing crunches on a mat by the barbells. She was shouting at him, chalked hands slapping her knees, a fervor in her sapphire eyes that reminded Parker of the sheen in her father's eye when he talked about hostile takeovers or billion-dollar mergers.

"Pick it up, Ace, what are you doing? Nana crunches? These the crunches your nana taught you? Your nana didn't care to sweat, huh? Didn't like the burn? I said, pick it up! There you go! Tell your nana how it hurts. Tell her how much you like that pain. Feel it! Come on, Ace!"

Rather than interrupt, Parker stood within the woman's periphery, shifting her weight from foot to foot, twirling her fingers around her purse string, waiting to be noticed. The longer she breathed in the stench of the gym, the more she found herself liking the smell. It was becoming familiar, almost comforting. She let her eyes roam the gym, taking in the men who worked in pairs around the space, benching weights or double-fisting the speedbag, grunting through pushups or showing off on the chin-up bar. No one was sparring in any of the rings, and whatever had been welling up in Parker's chest a while ago sank to the bottom of her stomach and lay there like a slab of bad fish.

"Great set, Ace. Hey, give me a sec here. Go grab some iron, but don't dick around with those one hundreds. Come on, man. Have some dignity." The woman patted the man on the butt in a comradely fashion and sent him on his way. To Parker, she popped her gum and smiled., "Hey, look at you, all spit-shined and pretty."

Parker shook her head in the miniscule way she'd been doing since middle school, so that her bangs fell over her face to hide her blush. "Yes, thank you. You...you work here?"

The woman laughed. "I train here," she corrected. "This place is mine. Victory's Training

Gym. I'm Victoria Marshall." She stretched a hand out to Parker, who shook it, not minding the grip powder that dusted her palm, and introduced herself in return.

"You got a solid grip there, Parker. You work out?"

Suddenly, Parker found herself back in the locker room, changing into a spare set of shorts and sneakers offered by Victoria, her plans to hermit inside her room for the rest of the day forgotten. Some part of her knew Victoria was only being kind, taking pity on her even, humoring a shy, shat-upon kiddo with a little attention for an hour or so. But it was more kindness and attention than her parents had shown her. She seemed shielded in here, too, from pooping birds, from school anxiety, from the disapproving eyes of her staff, from all of it. As she wrapped her knuckles with boxer's tape the way Victoria had showed her, she felt the grin returning to her face.

She worked the heavy bag with Victoria for a bit. The trainer praised the force of her jab and showed Parker how to space her legs and plant her feet to add more weight to her punches. She spotted Parker while she attempted to bench press, and then offered dumbbell curls to help her recover from the embarrassment of only being able to press the empty bar. She squeezed Parker's biceps, exclaiming "Nice!" and seeming to really mean it. After a round of sit-ups, push-ups, and chin-ups – none of which Parker could quite do to completion without help – Victoria offered Parker a bottle of water from the fridge behind the front desk, and asked if she wanted to join Victory's Training Gym.

"You got potential," she said. She nodded to a couple of guys who were leaving the gym, their arm muscles gleaming and taut. Parker looked askance at her own arms, which felt like throbbing noodles and just looked sweaty. "You interested in fighting? You got a fighter's build. There're some minor matches I could get you started in. Nothing fancy, small bit of prize money, maybe a write-up in a couple local papers. What do you think? Gotta ask the folks?"

Parker rooted in her purse and handed over her credit card. "I make my own decisions."

Victoria winked at her. "Hell yeah you do, kid." But when she swiped the card, the machine declined it. It declined the next two cards Parker offered as well. Her face flushed with embarrassment. Anger rushed up from her toes, stopping in her stomach to eat the rising ball of hope that had started to form there, before lodging firmly in her throat.

"Listen, don't worry about it. Today was on the house. Come back next week, maybe, after you talk with your–"

Parker poured out the contents of her purse and slammed the empty, fifteen-thousand-dollar Fendi bag on the counter. "What about a trade?"

Later that night, Parker talked to her father on the phone, who confirmed he'd cancelled her credit cards and she wouldn't be getting another dime until she agreed to start seeing a tutor and improve her grades.

"But Dad, grades are stupid," Parker argued. She would have sent crying emojis if this conversation had been a text, which it absolutely could have been. "Like, no one would even care about them if I was, like, a point guard or something on the basketball team."

Her father sighed, a deeply annoying puff of air that always hit Parker like a punch. "Are you a point guard or something on the basketball team?"

"No, but that's not—"

"Well until you are, you'll be seeing a tutor and getting those grades up. No child of mine is going to fail high school. High school, for Christ's sake." She could see him pinching the bridge of his nose with two fingers, shunting the cell between his chin and shoulder to reach for his highball glass.

"Okay, fine, whatever." Parker acquiesced. Then she thought, It isn't basketball, but it's something, something I'm better at than lacrosse already, something he could, maybe, be proud of. So she said, "But, um, Dad, I...I met this woman today who coaches boxing. We had a session, and I was really good, and—"

His derisive laugh caught her off guard. She didn't have time to throw up a forearm for a block. Victoria would be disappointed. "Boxing, Parker? What is America doing to you? Boxing is not, it's not, dignified. Feminine."

"But, Dad—" but Parker didn't have anything else to say, or at least no more will to say it.

"If you don't like lacrosse, what about, let's think," she heard the ice in his glass tink together as he swirled his drink, doing all the thinking for both of them. "Gymnastics. No, ice skating, or dance. You know what, I have a client in the States who can get you under the best gymnastic coach in Boston. Hang on, let me find his number."

So, over the next four years, Parker trained at her father's gym, doing just well enough at gymnastics not to be flatly kicked out. She improved her grades enough to graduate without disgracing the family name, and her father made her go to college and start dance, which she didn't totally suck at. She flew low enough under the radar for anyone – not her parents, not her brothers, not her gaggle of sort-of friends who didn't even know her name – to notice how often she broke a bone in her hand or face, how many bruises she collected along her arms and torso, how many midnight ice baths she requested from her staff. Parker would have gone on like this indefinitely – doing everything her family expected from her just well enough for them to leave her alone, while secretly following her passion, training night and day with Coach Vic at Victory's, racking up small-time wins and reveling in the respect she got from her fellow fighters – but for the fact that she was actually good at her sport. Really good. And it was only a matter of time before someone noticed.

Chapter Four

Parker woke up to a hot tongue slathering snow off her chin. Considering she had just been dreaming about training with her old coach, she was mildly disturbed by the sensation. She'd never thought about Victoria sexually, nor really cared for any sort of licking (above the waist) during her bedroom activities, so waking up to such a thing felt several kinds of wrong. She propped herself up on aching elbows, and hurked up strings of stomach bile onto her lap. The tongue quickly dropped from her face and slurped at the disgusting sno-cone on her legs.

Only one of Parker's eyes peeled open. The morning sun sawed through thick cloud cover, its rays shearing through slowly falling snow. When the wind gusted, the snow sheeted, and Parker shivered. She was covered in the stuff, which served as a kind of blanket during the night, but which now only felt wet and cold. Very, very slowly, she nudged her dog off her legs and stood up.

Davey, the dog, was a small black-and-brown terrier of unknown mix, bearded and with large, bushy eyebrows that gave him remarkable character. His age was also unknown, as Parker had rescued him from a dog fighting outfit a week or so after renting her room in Hekla Lake. He'd been used as a bait dog to rile the larger dogs into a frenzy, and as a result, he was missing half an ear, his entire tail, and one front leg. When the sheriff's office broke up the illegal ring in Mill Valley and advertised all of the rescued dogs were up for grabs at the county shelter, something in little Davey's eyes caught her attention: the pain, the fear, the loss. The regret, maybe. Probably just simple hunger.

In the beginning, he didn't have a name (the shelter dubbed him Sparky, but that was a bit too cutesy for a survivor of his magnitude). She thought about naming him after a Viking god, as she'd been coronated Hel: Odin, Thor, Loki. But growing up, she'd read a book about strong Norse women who lived by the phrase, "We hang our gods from trees." If anything, by surviving so valiantly, this little mutt had proven he could best gods. Parker wasn't familiar enough with mythology to find a god-killing figure there, but she remembered the Catholic Bible tale that made its way into secular popularity, that of the child David slinging a rock into the eye of Goliath, dropping the giant against all odds.

Of course, she had shut him up in the apartment last night before she left for the hunt, so she was surprised to see him out in the valley now, licking her awake. She was surprised, as well, to find herself out in the valley. She didn't remember falling asleep here. But she had plenty of bumps on her head to account for the memory lapse, and for the black out. Careful not to turn her body too sharply, lest all her loosened bones scrape against each other, Parker stepped lightly in a tight circle, surveying the valley. The ground was covered in at least two feet of snow that continued to flake from the sky. Here and there, she could see the tell-tale bulge of a feral hog she'd downed. Some of the shallower patches of snow were stained a dark, burgundy red where a hog's blood had soaked through. These ones had been felled by bullets from the rifles of Parker's fellow hunters.

It was odd that the fallen would still be here. Typically, a cadre of state and county workers rode through the carnage on their ATVs after a hunt, lugging carcasses onto their hitched trailers. It was illegal to keep your kills, and besides they weren't worth anything, nor useful to anyone. No one had come by to collect the bodies. No one had come by to find Parker, passed out on the ground, all but spooning the largest feral hog in the valley.

All at once, Parker remembered the explosion that presaged her final entanglement with the hog at her feet. Looking toward the national park, toward the mountain, all she could see were snow-limned firs, spruce and red pine. The sky, where it wasn't gray with clouds, shone clear and blue. She sniffed, but smelled only crisp air, mud, blood, and lemongrass (Davey's shampoo). Nothing burnt or burning.

Davey nipped at Parker's knee, rubbing his snoot against her shin. He wagged his butt and kicked circles through the snow, barking at her.

"All right, Davey, calm down, I'm okay." She started to bend to pat him, but the pain in her gut wrenched her back upright. "I don't know how you got out, but let's go back, okay? Mommy needs a bath."

Lying in the snow all night had been akin to taking an ice bath, which certainly helped keep the swelling of some of her injuries at bay, but Parker found that she was much more stiff than usual. Things inside her felt bent and crooked, tender, and too easily giving way. She had to shuffle through the valley back into town, letting Davey lead the way so he could use his noggin to knock open the farmer's gate that marked the edge of the village. She latched the gate behind her and continued down an alley toward a side street that wound its way to the pub.

She was grateful not to encounter anyone on the long slog back to her place. Although the sun was pretty high in the sky, the road was covered in snow, walkways and windows, too. Barbara Mountain Seeker was slacking on her plowing duties. The street was eerily quiet, and Parker listened to the twinkling trill of birdsong, the whistling of the light wind, the soft thrum of blood in her ears. The smells of Patty's BBQ were long gone, but her cart and smoker were still set up outside of the pub, the lot still choked with pickups, Jeeps, and beaters that had come over last night from the gym. Maybe today was a holiday Parker didn't know about, and everyone was sleeping in. Maybe the snowstorm had come on so suddenly that it caught the villagers unawares, and so people were stuck inside until they could get a plow up from Mill Valley.

Parker needed a bath, and a drink, a mouthful of ibuprofen, and all the pancakes, eggs, and bacon she could find. She felt like she could sleep for three more days, but the desire to get clean and warm in a hot soak spurred her onward. In her room, she slowly undressed, throwing everything in a corner by her nightstand. Davey hopped around on her unmade bed in the middle of the small space, tracking mud and grass and probably poop. She'd deal with that later. For now, she hobbled over to the minifridge, shoved a few slices of ham cold cuts in her mouth, and tossed the rest of the pack to Davey.

Her room above the pub was sparse but cozy, the walls wood-paneled, the floor swathed in patchy carpeting that was probably a shade of white thirty years ago, but was now a mottled gray. The radiator was one of those old, clanging metal jobbies that sat counterintuitively under a window, the pane of which was sealed in the encasement so that it didn't open. Aside from her bed, Parker had, in her main and only living space, a TV mounted on her dresser (the beefy kind with an antenna built-in and no cable hook-up), the aforementioned nightstand, under which was Davey's nest of pillows, blankets, and squeaky stuffed toys. Along the far wall she'd set up a folding card table and single plush recliner (a garage sale boon), and her microwave perched next to it atop the minifridge. Cattycorner to this were two doors, one leading to a closet that would have been cramped if Parker owned anything other than a parka and snow coveralls, and the other leading to the half bathroom where she could take a shit and brush her teeth in privacy. For the bath or shower, she had to leave her room and go down the hallway and hope one of the other tenants wasn't using the shared full bath above the stairs. Parker didn't really know any of the other villagers who lodged here, and she wasn't keen on meeting any of them on her way to or from doing her business.

On her way out of the room, Parker examined the apartment door. There were no marks on the inside of the door, but there were scrapes along the bottom on the outside, and deep gouges in the baseboards on the outer wall. A few scratches up near the doorknob. Now that she thought about it, when she'd returned just a moment ago, she hadn't unlocked the door to let herself into the room. But it had been closed, she was pretty sure; she'd twisted the knob. She must have forgotten to lock it last night. "Shit," she breathed, and scurried back inside to check on her stash of tournament money. Still there.

Parker closed Davey in this time, rattled the door a bit to make sure he couldn't nuzzle it open. She secured the bath towel around herself and clutched her shower caddy in front of her waist lest anything swing unseemly open. Her feet padded on the carpeted hall, the sound banging through the noiseless space. She stopped in front of the closed bathroom door and listened. Nothing. No sounds from behind that door, or from behind the three other closed doors into the other tenants' rooms.

She listened far longer than was normal. A creaking wall here, a rattling window pane there.

In the bath, Parker took inventory of her injuries. Every part of her was sore, but once she'd cleaned herself up, she could see far fewer scratches than she expected, and no outright gouging. Her eyebrow was starting to scab over from the fight earlier in yesterday's evening, her jaw was puffy and bruising, and her gums were soft to the tonguing where she'd lost the latest molar. Two fingers on her right hand were possibly broken; she'd splint them when she got back to her room. The bruising across her upper chest and collarbone looked like spidery black mold, but pressing a thumb to the tender places, while painful, did not shift any splintered bones around, so she could be confident that area was intact. Very sore ribs and tender, bruised flesh around her lower abdomen, but again, nothing broken. Her legs, especially her thighs where the feral hogs' butting heads easily reached, were so mottled with multicolored bruises they could easily be mistaken for athleisure tights.

All in all, not a bad feral hog hunt.

Parker scraped off blood from the defensive wounds on her forearms and biceps, scrubbed extra hard at the dirt and detritus under her fingernails, and soaked her head under the scorching hot water while making sure to wash out her ears, nostrils, and the creases of her face. When she peed in the toilet, it didn't hurt any more than the act of bending to sit on the pot, and no blood came out, so she figured there was no internal damage to her kidneys, despite the gnarly bruises. She wiped steam off the mirror and looked herself over before wrapping the towel back around her body. She looked rawer than she felt, and far less tired. At least she smelled better than she had in many hours.

Davey whirled in circles on her bed before finally settling down on top of her pillow to watch her get dressed. She pulled on a bra, boxer briefs, an oversized gray t-shirt and a pair of blue basketball shorts. She kicked the radiator, and it sputtered to life, puffing dust and the smell of burnt hair into the room, followed by hot air. Parker considered her stomach for a moment: it growled low, like one of the feral hogs she'd pummeled. But she was probably at least a few hours away from true hunger pangs, and the ache in her joints – temporarily relieved by the bath – proved to be the deciding factor in what Parker did next.

She pulled back the covers, flopped face first on her pillow beside Davey's bum, and fell – gloriously, ravenously – to sleep.

The first time she woke up, it was dark. She'd slept through the whole day. Davey had, at some point, gotten up and piddled by the door, and now looked, lying once again with his butt resting against Parker's cheek, at least slightly abashed. He buried his nose under his paw as she shook her head at him, a gesture that was more like a twitch considering how stiff her neck was. She rubbed at it, sitting up and looking out the window. It was darker than usual, even though she could see the moon, partially obscured by thick clouds moving quickly south. It was snowing, but the wind had died down. Parker heard an owl hooting, but not much else. No car sounds, no people sounds. She got up and leaned her face against the cold pane so she could see further. Out on the street, only the two automatic streetlights at either end of Main Street were on, illuminating a deep blanket of snow that covered, well, everything. No porch lights were on in any of the houses or apartments. She could tell from there being no glow on the snow below her window that no lights were on inside the pub, either. Jimmy's, and the garage next to it, was dark.

"Where is everyone, Davey?" The dog perked up his good ear at the mention of his name, but otherwise didn't stir.

Parker grabbed a bottle of water from the fridge and opened a couple bags of tuna, which, snuggled back in bed with Davey, she slurped straight from the pouch like a particularly bad stick of Go-Gurt. She let Davey lick the pouches clean and drained her water. Sated for now, she sank back against her headboard, lower back supported by one of her pillows, and thought a minute. It was too late to go out and ask around to see what was going on – why hadn't Mountain Seeker, or anyone else, plowed the village's streets? What happened to the clean-up crew that was supposed to come out after the hunt? Why weren't any of the late-night establishments open? Why had everyone allowed their vehicles to get snowed in, their walkways covered, their own doors and windows practically sealed shut with snow drifts? Where was everyone? But maybe she could text someone.

In her nightstand drawer, Parker retrieved her phone from its charger, and panned around for a signal. Even after she creakingly got out of bed, walked every foot of the room and half-bath, and even ventured into the eerily quiet hallway and down to the shared bath to search for a signal, she had zero bars. The storm must be obscuring the cell towers and satellite relays. Ditto the internet; it was out. She checked her messages and found the last one she got was two days ago: Jimmy, reminding her to bring her own whiskey to tomorrow's (yesterday's) tourney because he was tired of her stealing his hooch (she hoped for his sake, then, that he didn't check the toilet tank in the locker room, because then he'd have to mourn the loss of the fifth she'd jacked to help her deal with her broken tooth). When she scrolled through her contacts, she found she only had four numbers stored aside from Jimmy's: her landlord's, her father's, and Sylvie's.

Her father's number was in there so if it ever did show up on her caller ID – which, in a year and some change, it hadn't yet – she would know not to answer it. Her father didn't have this cell number, neither did anybody else from her past life, for that matter. Still, she kept his. Just in case.

Now, back in bed once again, she realized even if she could call someone who could shed a little light on this situation, she had precious few people she actually would. Not Kulla; he'd let it go to voicemail and wouldn't return her call unless it was about rent, or something broken in the apartment that no one in the village could fix as a favor for him. Not Jimmy; he would also let it go to voicemail, and wouldn't care to return her call unless it concerned an upcoming fight, or an idea about how to make more money at the next match, or if she was offering to replace the booze she'd been pilfering over the months of being his headliner. That left Sylvie, and even the thought of calling her – knowing she couldn't call her because there was no signal – made Parker queasy.

It wasn't that Parker didn't want to call Sylvie. Her fingers itched to, her flesh begged to, but her gut warned her against it. It would be awkward, she'd waited too long, said too many hurtful things when she decided to burn that blossoming friendship down to the studs. And then what would it mean – what would Sylvie think it meant, and what would it actually mean, and did Parker need to know what it meant or to explain what it meant, or did it have to mean anything at all anyway? People called each other. Acquaintances called each other, business partners called each other, strangers called each other. Calling each other wasn't just for friends, or for more-than-friends. It didn't matter anyway, because Sylvie didn't live in the village. If she was home, in Mill Valley, she wouldn't have the answers to any of Parker's pressing questions. Well, maybe she would know about the hunt, on account of her job, but she wouldn't be able to answer any of the other ones. And if she wasn't home, she'd be working, driving through the national park in her state-issued SUV, keeping an eye on the wildlife, or up in a fire tower, looking out for lost hikers or campers building illegal campfires or setting off fireworks for an ill-conceived gender reveal party. She'd be out of range even if there was a signal, and too busy to care about whatever the hell was happening in Hekla Lake.

But the biggest reason Parker didn't call her, or anyone else, right now – the reason she plugged the fully-charged phone back into the charger and closed it back up in the nightstand, and then curled up on her side and spooned herself around a snoring Davey – was because of the goddamn dream she'd had, passed out in the valley, about her former life.

Truthfully, and all evidence to the contrary these past twenty-four or so hours, Parker didn't spend too much time dwelling on the origins of her big, ugly mistake. Sure, she thought about the fallout, was living the fallout, as much as she didn't like to admit it. She thought about the immediate aftermath, and the pain and the shame and the loathing. But how it all began, everything that led up to the big, dumb, stupid, disgusting snafu – that, she didn't dwell on. Partly because it didn't matter – how could she have known where any of it was leading? How could those choices, before she met Guillermo "Ray" Reyes, at least, have directly led to what she eventually did? They couldn't have, and so Parker didn't dwell. But, mostly, she didn't dwell because they were good memories; training with Coach Vic, fighting amateur heavyweight boxing tourneys, collecting trophies and press and praise – those were the happiest moments of Parker's life, unmarred by the consequences of every choice she made after, starting with the choice to leave boxing and move into mixed martial arts.

Ray didn't propose trading in her golden gloves for grappling gloves right away, of course. No, that would have tipped his hand a bit too far, maybe made her ask more questions than the exactly zero that she did. He took her out to dinner following a big regional win, the first time a man had asked her out to dinner – the first time anyone had asked her out to dinner, except for Victoria and her wife, on occasion – and he knew it, made little jabs about it disguised as compliments ("Has anyone ever told you how pretty you are? When you do your hair like that and in that dress. Bet you don't have occasion to dress so fancy very often? I wish more men would see how pretty you can be, I truly do."). Parker, of course, blushed and twittered in all the right places, not only at the male attention, but because Guillermo "Ray" Reyes was kind of a big deal in the amateur sporting world.

"Guy's a sleaze," Coach Vic cautioned Parker a couple of days before their date was it a date? Parker blushed at the thought but couldn't shake it.

"You've said that before," Parker said. She slammed a jab-jab-hook into the heavy bag Coach held for her.

"And I'll keep saying it until it isn't true. Don't drop your shoulder like that, come on, you know better."

Parker danced on the balls of her feet, slapped her gloves together before trying the combo again, earning a grunt of approval from her coach. She panted, "I know you hate him. But he has connections, he can—"

Victoria interrupted, "—get you a big money deal, flashy cars, expensive perfumes, French cut velvet suits. Kid, he's been spinning his spiel since before you learned fractions." She relaxed her hold on the heavy bag, motioned for Parker to take a break. Parker squirted cold water over her head while Coach Vic went on, "You can make your own decisions, kid, but let me tell you something about good ol' Ray. He takes a larger cut than most managers, and he won't hesitate to pimp you out like his own personal whore. Don't pull that face with me, I'm just telling it true. He cares more about his oil-slicked used-car-salesman hair than he does about his athletes. Parker."

For a brief moment, Coach Vic held Parker's gaze tighter than she'd been holding the heavy bag. The laugh lines crinkling from the corners of her eyes deepened into tiny frowns. Her voice hardened as she told Parker, "Ray doesn't care about you."

But in the next beat, one of Coach Vic's featherweight students grabbed her for something, and Parker was left to finish her workout with only the butterflies in her gut for company. The desperate flapping of their wings drowned out Vic's words, and then their meeting – their date? – was happening, and Ray was telling her how much she could have, how much she'd deserve if she trained hard enough, bled red enough, and let Ray worry about networking with the fat white gatekeepers of her sport.

On that last point, Ray had things right. Rising through the echelon of amateur fighting, especially as a woman, meant schmoozing with old pot-bellied, balding, Mozzeralla-and-garlic smelling cheeseballs, who'd never fought in the ring but owned everyone who did. Ray wasn't a white guy, or old, and he smelled good and worked out (though he'd never fought), so Parker immediately trusted him more than the other dons. Sure, he wore fat, gold rings on every other finger, had platinum teeth, and used too much pomade. But his smile was warm, his grey eyes enticing, his skin so soft it barely hurt when he back-handed Parker with compliments. She knew if he agreed to take her on, he could get her some real fights, where she could go up against men (it was difficult to find women in the heavyweight division whom she hadn't already roundly destroyed between the ropes), earn some real clout. She didn't care so much about the prize money – although she did tuck it away in an account untouchable by her family, should her father ever decide to throw another tantrum and freeze her debit cards. But the prestige, the relative fame, the aplomb and respect – the approval – of her peers and her mentors alike – those things, she desperately craved.

So after Ray wined and dined her, kissed her hand goodnight when he dropped her off at her apartment (so it was a date!), and she'd told Coach Vic all about their "business meeting," listening half-heartedly to Coach voice her concerns again, Parker didn't hesitate to respond, "YESS!!" when he texted to ask if she wanted to meet for a drink to discuss a career opportunity. It was during the drinks that he pitched his idea for her to join MMA; if she let him – that's how he phrased it – so humble, let him be her manager, he would get her the best MMA trainers, the best nutritionists; she'd get fights against people of all genders, as the weight divisions were less stringent, and she'd travel, staying in the best hotels, fighting televised matches, pay-per-view, on-demand cable. He'd take a big cut in the beginning, to offset the costs of everything he was setting her up with, but after she won a title or two, her take would double, triple, skyrocket! He'd get her face on the cover of every industry magazine, articles in wider sports publications, features on blogs and websites.

"Besides," he chucked her chin up with a gentle knuckle, caught her in the center of his storm gray eyes. "I think I'm falling in love with you, Parker." He pressed his mouth to hers, right outside the restaurant, before they'd even got into his car, where everyone could see. He tasted like the sugar from the rim of his margarita glass. He tasted like destiny.

After the kiss, he held her close and whispered wetly into her ear, "You're mine, baby girl. Let's make this work, you and me, baby girl. You and me." She had never known romance like this.

Parker told her parents – who had finally found out about her fledgling boxing career after she won a high-profile regional tournament and one of her father's business partners sent him a clipping from a popular American newspaper – about the offer Ray had made, not to seek advice but really, kind of, sort of, to gloat. To her shock, they were excited for her, even her mother, who wanted to know when her first MMA bout was so the family could book tickets to fly in and see her. After that call went so well, Parker soundly avoided talking to Coach Vic in person. She knew Vic wouldn't approve. So instead, she wrote an all-too-brief note, slipped it into the gym's mailbox, and left.

She moved to Las Vegas and into an apartment with Ray. Their relationship was passionate and joyful in the beginning, but the more Parker won – the harder she trained with her coaches, the more attention she got from the media, the more money she raked in to buy Ray's diamond-encrusted fillings – the meaner Ray got. He never hit her, but he implied often enough that she was lucky he didn't that she was constantly on edge. She knew she could take him in a fight, but the way his body tensed, the way his eyes deadened, the veins in his neck twitched...He looked like a cornered animal, gearing up for a frenzied counterattack against someone invading its territory. But Parker wasn't invading Ray's territory; he invited her here, and every win she got also got him attention, money, more power in the old-white-guy world he bulldozed his way through.

She figured she just had to work harder to show him she loved him. That's why, when he told her she needed to start letting other fighters win against her, she didn't question it. The way he explained it, it made sense, to that frayed part of her brain that tore itself apart with the desire to please men. She had to show she was not totally untouchable, give the guys some hope of victory, let them feel like men every now and again. Too much emasculation was bad for everyone, because if she won too much, no one would want to fight her. She'd cease to be a challenge and become an annoyance. They'd start to ignore her, decline invites to fight her, stop inviting her to special events. So, she needed to give a little, in order to get a little. Parker could understand that. She started throwing matches with a smile on her swollen face.

Things got better again, and then they got worse, and then they came to a head. Parker was set to take on MMA Champion Carter Max in a national title bout for the American Fighter's Federation (AFF) heavyweight belt. It was a super high-profile event, and she'd worked hard for over a year with her trainers and Ray, maneuvering herself into position to challenge Max. She had enough clout at this point that she was a real contender, not a token fighter thrown in the mix to spice things up, raise ratings and bloat ticket sales. She had pumped herself up, despite the hardships she faced at home; she knew she could win this, would win this, and then everything would be different. She'd attain a whole new level of prestige, and many doors in the MMA world would open for her. Probably, she thought, she'd dump Ray, become a manager or a trainer herself, start her own training gym, get her rocks off in a novelty bout every now and then. Retire a legend, a celebrity in her own right, and reap the spoils while she was still young enough to enjoy them.

But then, Ray came to her right before the match and told her she needed to throw the fight.

Parker's stomach dropped out of her butt. "What?"

She'd been pacing the large private locker room, set up more like Parker imagined a green room on a movie set: all fine leather seating, a huge vanity with every grooming implement known to man, flower arrangements everywhere, an edible bouquet softly dripping melon juice onto a stainless-steel end table. The lighting was dim, there were rugs and tapestries. A team of hair and make-up people had just whirled out of the room, and she was waiting for her trainer to give her one last pep talk, assure her all the pomp was for the cameras and not because no one actually took her seriously. But then Ray walked in, and said–

"You heard me, baby girl." His face was grim, lips curled over his platinum teeth. His collar was up, starched stiff as a board, his cerulean velvet jacket making him perspire. In one hand, he gripped a half-smoked cigar like a weapon.

The hackles on the back of Parker's neck stood up. He was facing her down like a contender, not like his girlfriend. She relaxed her shoulders, loosened her limbs, tried to smile. "I don't understand, Ray—"

"You don't need to understand, sweetness," he slid toward her. "You just gotta obey. Give Max a few rounds, don't make it look sloppy. Open your back to him, let him take you out at the kidneys." He shrugged, as if it would be easy. So easy, to throw everything away.

Parker couldn't find words. She could barely find breath. But her hesitation was resistance enough. Ray closed the gap between them, fisted Parker's chin in his hand. The etchings on his rings left impressions in her skin.

"Chin up, baby girl," he said through clenched teeth. His face was so close to hers, she could see the anger twitching through him like a parasite. Spittle vibrated on his bottom lip. "This is still your moment. Our moment. We cash in, we move on. But, hey." He squeezed so hard Parker's mouth popped open with an audible clack. She held in her wince, hoping a bone in her jaw would crack just to feel some relief. "I can always leave you, you know.

Would you like that? You can be over, sweetness, finished in MMA forever. No one will touch you if I say so. You're mine, remember?"

He eased up, drew on his cigar, blew the smoke into her slack mouth. "So be a good girl."

As she walked down the corridor to the MMA cage, cheers and stomping feet exploding around her, camera flashes blinding her, smiling through her mouthguard, Parker didn't know what she was going to do. But when she climbed over the ropes, and stared at the opposite corner at her opponent as he held his championship belt over his head and paraded around for the crowd, Parker slowly gathered up the innards that had descended out of her in the locker room and shoved them back inside. She took a slow turn to scope out the crowd herself, and saw in the front row – where even her parents had stopped coming to matches after her first fight, claiming to catch them on TV – stood Coach Vic, her wife, and their two teenage kids. Vic's hands were cupped around her mouth, shouting along with the crowd. Maybe she imagined it, maybe she wanted it so badly she manifested it, but however it happened, she heard it – Vic's voice, imploring, "Give him hell, kid!"

Parker tightened her stomach, puffed her chest, and held her chin high. She couldn't throw this match. She wouldn't. She would win.

Parker won, and then she was beaten to within an inch of her life on her way home that night. Ray disappeared while the ref was still holding her victorious arms aloft and the announcer was shouting amazement into the microphone to the cacophonous elation of the crowded arena. When she couldn't find Ray afterward, she changed into her street clothes, and left the gym out the backway to avoid the press. She remembered being hit from behind with something heavier than a fist, and she remembered vomiting on someone's blurry leg around the third or fourth time they kicked her in the stomach, while her own arms were held behind her in a vice-like grip. She woke up in a hospital bed, choking on a feeding tube, mummified in bandages, tubes and needles and all manner of things pumping and beeping and keeping her alive. Perhaps she was beaten to death but revived; she didn't really pay attention to what the doctor said. Her father took care of things, and whisked her home, to Trondheim, when she was well enough to travel.

It was there, still on bedrest in her family's palatial estate – kept company by the staff as her parents and siblings jet-setted about – that Parker finally logged onto the internet or flipped the TV to a news station. That's when she was greeted by pictures of her own face, unworldly happy following her win, pasted next to Guillermo "Ray" Reyes being escorted in handcuffs into a police vehicle, underneath headlines decrying Ray as a swindler, a fraud, an embezzler and a cheat, and touting Parker as his latest patsy.

The articles all described the same scenario: that the FBI had been investigating Ray for years, that he was basically involved in insider-trading-level scandals within MMA and other amateur sporting circles; he placed large back-alley bets against his own athletes and then had them throw their matches. Been doing it for so long without negative consequences that he got cocky, placed a bloated bet against Parker in her title bout with Carter Max, a match dangerously high-profile for such shady dealings. He probably would have been caught even if she'd done as he commanded and thrown the fight, but things turned out worse for him when she won: he lost big, big big, and he turned himself over to the FBI, confessed to everything, in exchange for their protection against whomever he owed. (Most likely the very same individuals who had tried to kill Parker herself.)

It took days for this revelation to settle into Parker. She felt like a ratty old sponge, at once too porous to retain the onslaught of news she clicked and flipped through, but grievously lapping up every last morsel as a matter of course. Finally, after having exhausted all her news source options, but still not quite believing everything she read and watched, she used her family's contacts to track down where Ray was being detained, and she called him.

"I knew you'd call, baby girl." Ray's voice was distant, garbled by static. Parker had to close her eyes and remind herself how far away he was, how his naked fingers were curled around a phone cord behind feet of cement and barbed wire, not around her neck. Ray said into her silence, "Your pops finally come clean?"

The question snapped her bruised eyes open. "What?" She couldn't get out any more than that.

Laughter from Ray almost made Parker's heart stop. "You kidding me? You gotta be the dumbest bitch I ever fucked." His snarl bit into her ear, but she couldn't put the phone down. Couldn't hang up. Couldn't leave Ray even now.

"Your pops, man. He's something else. Don't get me wrong, a great dad, but a scoundrel, a real piece of shit, baby girl. Yeah, good ol' daddy was the guy who sold you to me in the first place." Laughter thrummed through the static, through the rush of blood in Parker's head. "What, you think I offered you a gig because you were just that fucking good? In and out of the sack, that's wildly untrue. You were desperate, your pops had cash. Show me a guy who wouldn't take you both for a ride and I'll sell you some ocean-front property in Wyoming."

Stop. But she didn't say it out loud. Her jaw felt wired shut again. She pressed the button to release the morphine drip into her IV and waited to float away.

"You know, he even bought your opponents. Did you really think any man wanted to fight you? Come on now, sweetness, you can't be that stupid. No guy wants to fight a woman, that's sideshow shit. But leave it to father dearest, he paid off more managers and refs than I ever have. I mean, I coulda learned from him. Him and me, we coulda been the real team. But nah, he fucked me over. Fucked you over too, baby girl. How d'you think you won against ol' Maxipad, huh? You think you're just so fucking good, you can take a goddamn heavyweight champ? Come on, bitch, your pops bet big on you and then slipped Max a little something to throw the whole thing. Double-crossed the shit out of me, that son of a bitch. And here I am, brown man in jail, while King White Guy rides the whole thing out in his Scandinavian castle. Look at us, baby girl. You and me still got something in common, don't we? We're dopes, idiots both, and don't we fucking hate ourselves for it. You do hate yourself, don't you, baby girl?"

She did. And she hated Ray, and she hated her father, and she hated, hated, hated Victoria, who convinced her she was anything at all, could be better and better and better, and then let her go and prove her so remarkably wrong. The anger seethed through her, burning across her muscles like a salve, healing her aches and lingering pains with its fire. Before her family returned from whatever sojourn they were on, Parker fled. She packed light and she left her father's credit cards behind. Even though most of the money in her own account was dirty – attained as her boyfriend's patsy, her father's poker chip – it was at least hers. She'd earned it one way or another, by her fists and her blood and all her disastrously wasted years. She took a plane back to America, bought a cheap car, and drove until she figured out what to do next, which turned out to be bury herself, punish herself, reclaim some speck of self-esteem, in a small nothing mountain town on the border of a national park where she could beat herself up in peace and tranquility.

Thinking about all of this weighed Parker down. She set aside her useless phone, blocked out the strangeness of the past twenty-four hours, the unearthly quiet of the village. She felt like an overwhelmed teenager again; she wanted to crawl back to the bath and sink into the hot water, but even entertaining the idea of getting up was exhausting. After so many hours dredging up the habits of her past to get her through whatever the hell was happening in her present, what was one more? She pulled the covers to her chin, curled up around Davey – already snoring and farting in equal measure – and willed herself back to sleep.

Chapter Five

After too much sleep, Parker decided she needed to balance things out with some action, or risk atrophying in her bed. She donned her gear and went exploring.

Rooting through the village council members' desk drawers didn't turn up anything useful, but it was mildly entertaining. For instance, Cheryl Henry had a secret and quite extensive collection of troll dolls in her bottom drawer, whose multicolored hair she clearly fussed with on a daily basis. Martin Tiger, the chief council member and essentially the mayor of Hekla Lake, had an entire file cabinet full of miniature liquor bottles, the kind you typically get at the airport. This in itself wasn't surprising or unique, but he'd also taken to outfitting each one in its own hand-sewn Hawaiian shirt, like a wine bottle cover but weirder. Stephanie Allen, the final council member, didn't have anything untoward or interesting in her desk. The closest thing to odd was maybe the full legal notebook pad she'd darkened with variations of her signature. Perhaps a nervous habit, or just her way of doodling idly during village community meetings.

The council members' office was in a dedicated room of a three-room community building. The other two rooms provided space for non-denominational church or tribal services, monthly village community meetings, occasional indoor sports meet-ups, birthday or holiday parties, and pretty much anything for which a villager needed the space, provided the date and time were available on the sign-up sheet. It was the second place Parker searched for answers after she'd knocked on seven or eight residential doors and gotten no response – not even a barking dog or squawking finch – on her way down Main Street.

With nothing to show for her effort, Parker, wearing snowshoes and her winter coveralls and parka, clomped through waist-high snow out to where the road curved and began to descend the mountain, away from Hekla Lake, and down toward Mill Valley. Maybe there were people in Mill Valley – maybe Hekla's villagers were there, having the forethought to batten down the hatches in the sheltered valley to wait out the snowstorm. But they would have boarded up their homes, taken their vehicles or at least moved them into garages or under carports, and someone would have told Parker about this plan. Right?

It didn't really matter if anyone in Mill Valley could offer some insight. It took Parker damn near two hours to trudge the mile down Main Street to the bend in the road; she'd never make it the twenty more miles to Mill Valley in these conditions. Moving through the unplowed road was like swimming against a current; she butterflied her arms in front of her to clear a path and then clomped her snowshoes down to flatten the cleared space. After realizing she wasn't going to be able to get down the mountain this way, she worked her way over to the community hall building, hoping to find some sort of disaster or emergency plan in the village council members' desks that would explain where everyone was.

Finding nothing useful, Parker pocketed as many tiny bottles of alcohol as she could carry, and went back outside. She did stop first to drink from the water fountain in the main room, which still worked, so at least it wasn't cold enough for the water pipes to have frozen. The heating in the hall kicked on automatically, so that most likely accounted for it. Some of the residences and smaller businesses in the village wouldn't be so lucky.

Outside, it was still snowing and the sky was grey. There was no sun to warm things up or start melting some layers of snow, which was probably for the best anyway. Melting snow froze to ice overnight, and getting around would become even more treacherous. As it was, even though it was only mid-afternoon, Parker thought she should head back to her apartment as it would be getting dark by the time she got there. Davey was waiting for her, and she could warm up, feed Davey and herself, and figure out what to do next. She would have to call Sylvie, if she could get a signal. If anyone could help her, it would be the ranger.

Parker pulled out her cell phone, used her teeth to remove her glove, and thumbed the power button. She held it aloft and moved it around, but still there was no signal. Cursing, she shoved the phone back in her parka pocket, tugged her glove back on, and adjusted her hood around her head. She was plenty warm everywhere except for her face, which was dried out and starting to sunburn, despite the overclouded sky.

She'd only made it about ten steps down the path she'd carved through the snow on her way out to the community hall when an animal's anguished bleating stopped her cold. She looked out past the single-story homes that curved down Whitman Road, straining to listen. After a few seconds, there it was again: the cry of something in pain. It was coming from one of the homesteads on the west edge of town.

Parker didn't give it a second thought. She abandoned her pre-carved path home, and wrestled her way through the snow, toward the animal's SOS call.

It was dark by the time she reached the farm. She saw the cow right away: it was a mother, keening over her calf, who lay impaled and unmoving on a jagged piece of broken fence. Parker kept her distance, not only to catch her breath and rest her arms and legs – which throbbed and moaned with her hours of effort – but to assess the situation.

The broken fence surrounded Barbara Mountain Seeker's property, a thirty-eight-acre plot where she and her spouse, Kevin, grew tobacco, cannabis, and tomatoes. They also raised cows, goats, and sheep for their milk, which Mountain Seeker used to create artisanal cheeses and soaps. In the field nearest Parker, where the cow mourned, there was a small barn adjacent to a second grazing field. Beyond that were the crop fields and a decent-sized greenhouse, all covered by snow. If Parker followed the fence down the dirt road, she'd come to the house, which she could just make out in the dark, with a little garage and carport. Under the carport, shining like a beacon, was Mountain Seeker's truck, plow inertly attached to the frontend.

As much as Parker wanted to sprint toward the plow, she restrained herself. Several dark shapes moved about in the two grazing fields. She had to round up the remaining livestock, get them tucked away in the barn before the snowstorm renewed itself and they died of exposure, or escaped through the broken fence.

She approached the mother cow, head low, and stayed in the cow's eyeline. As she neared, she saw that the calf was half covered in snow and there was no blood on the white blanket; the little thing must have tried to get over or through the fence before the snow had fully fallen, suffered its injury and loped back toward the barn, but collapsed before it could make it. Mother Cow probably stumbled upon it, and now could not be consoled. Parker briefly wondered what, if anything, the calf had been running from to try to leap over or bust through the fence. Any evidence of predators in the area – tracks, fur, teeth – were disappeared by the snow. Anything could have happened. Parker wouldn't find any answers waiting for the calf to pop back to life and tell her about it.

It took some convincing, but Parker finally coaxed the cow, through a combination of soft coos and brute strength, away from the calf and back to the barn. They followed the path the cow had already beaten through the snow, even though it zigzagged around in circles. Parker was too bone-tired to swim a new path, so she meandered, herding another few cows and a couple goats along her way. She got everyone penned up in the barn, filled their troughs with water and what feed she could find, and shut the barn doors tight. She noticed deep grooves at about knee height in the wood of the doors, scratches further up near the crossbar, similar to what she'd seen on her own apartment door. Peculiar, but she dismissed it for now. She turned and scanned the grazing fields but didn't see any more moving shapes. The handful of sheep Mountain Seeker owned were lost or dead, buried under the snow or carried off by whatever had made those grooves in the barn doors or scared the calf into fleeing for its life.

The feral hogs, Parker thought wildly, but she shook the thought away. The hogs never made it into the village. The mountains kept them away from this side, and their only entry through the valley was wide open; under normal circustances, if they did try to stream into the village, someone would see and either take care of it themselves or sound the alarm. Everyone in town owned at least one rifle, and even what few kids there were knew how to shoot, and knew the danger feral hogs posed. There were other far more likely culprits, especially if Mountain Seeker had been raptured like the rest of town, leaving their livestock vulnerable.

As Parker pushed her way through the snow toward the house and the truck, she considered the possibility of the rapture. She wasn't even a little bit religious, but she'd watched enough end-of-the-world movies to be a little bit anxious about the prospect. What if everyone in the village had been raptured, culled into Heaven by the Almighty Himself? Maybe not just the village, but everyone in the neighboring towns and cities, in the state, in the nation, or the world? Only the sinners were left behind, to languish over their misdeeds, doomed to roam through Hell on Earth before their mortal bodies gave up and their souls shot straight down into the great fire below.

It wasn't hard for Parker to believe she'd be left behind in the rapture. Her sins were numerous, and she deserved the suffering. Still, over the fistful of months she'd lived in Hekla Lake, she'd gotten to know a number of its citizenry, if only superficially. There was no way she was the only sinner in the bunch.

Parker reached the carport and took refuge beneath the awning. It shielded her from the snow, large flakes falling harder now, and from some of the wind, which pierced her exposed face like diving icicles. After catching her breath and stretching a bit, she tried the driver's side door and felt it give, but she had to put some muscle behind it to tug it open, frozen as it was. Inside the cab, she slumped against the tarnished leather seat, and gave herself permission to close her eyes and rest for a moment. When her breathing returned to normal and feeling returned to her toes and fingers, she opened her eyes and dropped the sun visor. The keyring fell into Parker's lap. Parker would have smiled if her face wasn't stiff from sun and windburn.

Elation left Parker in a woosh when she keyed the ignition and the engine didn't kick over. There were a few sad clicking sounds, and the dashboard lights blinked once, but then nothing. She pumped the gas pedal and tried again but there was even less response this time. She waited several impatient minutes and then tried again. Nothing.

Instead of crying, Parker yelled. The hollow space of the cab filled up with her screams, with the padded pounding of her gloved fists against the steering wheel. When she was finished, she rooted around in the cab for anything else that might be useful. She found and chugged two unopened bottles of water that were slushy but not completely frozen and scarfed half an open bag of stale Cheetos. Sated for now, she chased her disappointment with the last of the water, and decided to see what was in the garage.

The carport was connected to the garage, so she didn't have to expend energy wading to it or clearing snow from in front of the door, situated beside the roll-up car entryway. As she suspected, and was grateful for, it was unlocked. No mysterious gouges or scuff marks, either. And it was warmer than inside the cab. She switched on the overhead light, and then she did cry. Because there in the middle of the garage was Mountain Seeker's snowmobile, a shiny Plan B that brought Parker, weeping, to her knees. She felt like genuflecting, throwing her head back and speaking in tongues, but she composed herself. She got up and inspected the Ski-Doo.

The keys were in the ignition, and it turned over with a beautiful roar that ebbed into a delectable purr. Parker shouted her triumph, her vibrato knocking a few tools off their wall pegs. But then she eyed the gas gauge: the needle was on empty, the light glaring at her like an evil eye.

"Fuck," Parker sighed.

After a bit of rummaging, she found two large red gas cans in the bed of the pickup, sickeningly empty. There was no gas station in Hekla, and the dregs that were left in the snowmobile wouldn't get her even halfway through the twenty miles down the mountain to Mill Valley. She chewed her lip and thought, but her brain was as sore and tired as her aching limbs. There had to be something she could do, somewhere she could go for help, with the aid of the snowmobile. It had maybe ten miles in it, give or take. Parker thumbed on her phone to check her GPS before remembering the storm had knocked out all internet access. Cursing, she was about to chuck the useless device into the snow when she caught sight of Sylvie's name, and her overworked mind alighted onto an idea.

The fire tower in the national park.

Sylvie told her it was stocked with all manner of emergency supplies, including a satellite radio that would no doubt be strong enough to call for help.

She was certain the snowmobile had enough gas to get her out to the tower, especially if the snowfall was lower in the forest, sheltered as it was by the trees' canopy of branches. She could get to the tower, radio the ranger station at the base of the mountain, and get someone to come get her and Davey. They'd figure out what the hell was going on in Hekla Lake after they were safely among other humans again. As much as she was used to being alone, she'd never been this alone, and it was kind of starting to freak her out.

Comforted by her new plan, Parker let herself into Mountain Seeker's house, helped herself to a few mini bottles of liquor she'd procured, peeled off her snow-drenched clothes, and crashed out on the softest, warmest couch she'd ever experienced.

At first light, Parker set out for her apartment. Or, rather, at first light after she brewed a pot of coffee, made herself scrambled eggs and bacon on an actual stove top, took a hot shower with optimal water pressure, and changed into a pair of Kevin's fleece-lined jeans, pullover hoodie, and fresh socks (all of which were too small for her, but she made it work with grit and some twine she fished out of a kitchen junk drawer). She helped herself to a couple swipes of Mountain Seeker's deodorant before she left the house. If Mountain Seeker was alive, and not raptured or carried off by some sort of Chupacabra, Parker figured she would buy her a round at the pub to pay her back for the stuff she borrowed.

The day was bright and mildly warmer than yesterday, with no windchill and no falling snow. Frost covered everything, sparkling like diamonds across the fresh layer of snow that had fallen overnight. String up some lights and erect a giant pine tree in the village square, and Hekla Lake was a winter wonderland. The quiet was unsettling, as was the absent scent of woodburning stoves and newly lit furnaces. Crunching through the snow toward the barn was like banging wildly away at a drumkit.

After ensuring the livestock was still secured, Parker hopped on the snowmobile and puttered back to the pub. She cruised down slopes when she could, not wanting to waste gas. At her apartment, she scooped up Davey, who was gravely annoyed to have been left alone so long, and peed and shat his indignation all over her comforter. She quickly outfitted him in his rugged tactical vest and snow boots, ordered special for him because goddamn it was cute (the extra snow boot she stored in a bedazzled keepsake box under her bed, whose other contents included the flyer for her first title bout at Jimmy's, the receipt from her first round of drinks with Sylvie, and two of her own teeth).

Parker stored her snowshoes, an extra coat, gloves, dry socks, a gallon of water, and a bag of dog treats in the snowmobile's saddle bags. She slid behind the handlebars, and Davey leapt onto her lap, as if he'd done this a thousand times. Parker tightened her snow goggles, kicking herself for not purchasing Davey a matching pair, and keyed the ignition. They set out for the forest through the valley, nudging the gate open with the nose of the snowmobile. The lumpy outlines of feral hog carcasses could no longer be made out underneath the snow of the past two days. It was slow going through the valley, but nowhere near as much of a crawl as slogging through on foot would have been. They picked up speed when they hit the forest, the snow less high and dense here, the sound of the snowmobile's engine exaggerated by the empty stillness between the trees.

When they reached the fire tower, Davey barked and bounded to one of the posts to mark his triumph with piss. Parker sat on the snowmobile a moment longer, engine off. The gas light's red glare seemed to deepen before she shut it off, warning her this was it; she'd been lucky so far, but just try to make a return trip, I dare ya. She listened to the stillness, head jerking toward any minute rustling or small animal chirps. Although she heard nothing out of the ordinary this far into the forest, her skin prickled with gooseflesh. She felt watched, stalked. She squinted into the trees but there was nothing there.

Parker dismounted, tucked Davey under her arm, and ascended the ladder to the tower's hut. It was a good hundred feet up, but the wooden rungs hadn't iced over, and carrying Davey, it was actually a welcome workout, one that didn't involve dodging blows or swimming through snow drifts. At the top, she lifted Davey in, and then hoisted herself over the threshold.

The lookout hut was roofed and walled, but the walls didn't connect to the roof, allowing three-hundred and sixty degrees of open sightline to the national park. A light dusting of snow had wafted in, and it was colder up here, owing to the wind, which gusted at intervals, shaking the tops of the forest's trees and eliciting unnerving creaks from the tower itself. There was a rudimentary desk and shelving against the far wall of the space, as well as a canvas camping chair a tall ranger could sit in while they scanned their surroundings. On the desk, Parker found a camo-green thermos partially full of old, stinky coffee, a pair of ranger's binoculars, a battery-powered camping lantern, and leather-bound logbook, filled in with a ranger's shorthand that Parker could not decipher. On the shelves, there was a large first aid kit, a couple gallons of potable water, packs and packs of batteries inside a weatherproof case, and the thing Parker came up here for: the satellite radio.

Parker removed her gloves (one of which Davey snagged off the low desk and curled up to chew) and switched on the radio. The display lighted up and static crackled. She fiddled with the dials and nobs until the static resembled that of an open landline from days gone by. She held down the "talk" button.

"Um, does anyone copy?" She asked the static. She released the button and listened for a response, but none came. "SOS," she tried again. "SOS, does anyone copy?"

She switched through channels, calling out her SOS, listening to the terrible static, until finally a voice like God's broke through.

"This is ranger station A6, we copy. Where are you?"

Parker whooped, causing Davey to bark, and then pressed the button down. "Great, okay, I'm not, I'm not a ranger, I'm coming from Hekla Lake, um, the fire tower on the southern face of Mount Shafah."

The static went on longer than was comfortable, but the voice returned before Parker's anxiety made her start to sweat. "Okay, we got you, you said this was an SOS? Who are you?"

"Yes, I don't know what's going on, but after the storm rolled in, the snowstorm, everyone is just...gone. Like, there's no one here, literally no one in the whole village, and it's weird, and, I don't know, I think something happened to everyone. I don't know what happened, but something happened. I can't make it down the mountain by myself, but I'm by myself, and god...god, it's just good to hear another voice."

The wave of emotion caught Parker by surprise, and she cut herself off before she started sobbing into the speaker. She coughed instead, and looked out at the forest, up at the mountain and along the skyline. Dark clouds were amassing again, another assault from the storm on its way.

"Okay, we hear you," came the voice. "That is strange. Look, we're going to send a helicopter out your way to check things out, but I don't have an ETA on arrival, okay? Are you hurt? Do you need medical attention?"

"No, I'm—" But Parker's thumb slipped off the button as her jaw gaped open at what she saw down below, slithering between the trees like cancer through a vein. Big, brown, toothy feral hogs, moving low to the ground, their snorting muffled but audible in the otherwise still forest. Their movements were coordinated as they rooted around methodically – no, not rooting; they were hunting. And they were zeroing in on a particular red pine.

Parker swiped the binoculars off the desk and pressed them to her eyes. Something was in the tree, obscured by the branches and the poor focus on the lens. She let the radio fall to the desk – the voice was speaking again, but Parker ignored it – and adjusted the lens until the blurry image crystallized and Parker saw – holy shit. Sylvie Cahwee. She was naked, clawing her nails into the tree trunk, her bare feet struggling to keep purchase on thin branches, her scratched-up thighs hugging the trunk.

As Parker watched, too stunned to move, the feral hogs circled closer, until, at the base of the tree Sylvie straddled, their snorting grew louder. They started throwing their bodies into each other, seemingly celebrating, before they pawed at the ground, scuffing the trunk, and drove their tusks into the bark, slamming the tree from all sides. In its branches, Sylvie shook and slid down by inches, scrambling. Parker heard her cry out, and the cry unstuck the binoculars from her face, nipped at her ankles as she ran to the ladder, chewed its way down her spine as she descended faster than was safe, and gripped her knuckles as she keyed on the snowmobile.

She plowed into the first of the eight hogs that surrounded Sylvie's tree. It made an anguished noise Parker found she actually missed as it flew through the air. Its body slammed into another tree, snow cascading from its shaken branches. She had the presence of mind to flip the engine off before dismounting, and then another hog bucked into the backs of her knees. She leapt onto the snowmobile's seat and pivoted. She launched a kick at the hog's maw, connected with its frothing snout. It backed up, replaced by one of its brethren. She bent and grabbed one tusk with both hands, planted a boot between its eyes and wrenched until a cracking split the air and the elongated tooth pulled free. The hog's eyes went wide and it bawled, loping off to nurse its shame. Parker wrapped her fist around the tusk's girth, held it pointy end downward, and leapt into the swarm of swine.

She landed on one's back, buckling its legs. Streaks of black fur underlined this one's eyes like war paint, fortuitously giving Parker something to aim at. As the beast writhed beneath her and its brethren croaked expletives through their snorts, she stabbed the thing through the eye with its buddy's broken tusk. It shrieked and bucked, and she let the tusk go as she fell to the snow-softened ground. The hog made it a couple of wild steps before keeling over at the hooves of its allies.

Parker felt suddenly as if she were surrounded by a pack of ravenous timber wolves, which was somehow worse than facing off against a handful of feral hogs. She had to shake off this image; there was no reason she should lose this fight. She regularly took down thirty to fifty of these guys every few weeks since she learned about the hunts, she could certainly handle eight of them (especially given one was dead, and she'd already injured three others). Yes, her body was a bit more battered, broken, and bruised than when she normally went toe to hoof with these guys, but the pain buoyed her; she channeled her suffering into rage, and released it on her opponents.

Her back to the tree, Parker heard Sylvie scrambling to keep her grip on the trunk, her feet from dangling too low off the branch she sat on. She panted and whimpered, but she wasn't crying or screaming anymore, and that seemed like a good sign to Parker.

The forest grew still, as if holding its breath. The hogs pressed in, creating a tight, semi-circle. A well-fed bunch, roughly two-hundred pounds apiece, the slightest one maybe a cool buck-fifty. In her mind, she dubbed this one Featherweight. They were all primarily brown, black-tipped tails and ears, frothy, slavering mouths and yellowing tusks. One hog's tusks curled inward, like a ram's horns, so she dubbed this one Ram. The hog whose tusk she'd dismembered stuck its marred face into the semi-circle, and she called him Ol' Onesie. A big guy with a blood stain across its snout like a birthmark: Port Wine. The one she'd booted in the nose from the seat of the snowmobile: Smush Face. The one that was more jowls than tusks: Jowly (a bit obvious, but she was kind of in a hurry). Finally, the one she'd plowed into had recovered, and limped into place among the seething ring of feral hogs. She called it Hit N' Run.

"Fellas," she nodded, breaking the silent spell. Recognition seemed to flash into their eyes as she took her fighting stance. While she was imagining things, Parker let herself believe the hogs' eyes also glistened with a healthy dose of fear. "I want a clean fight, okay?"

Ram grunted out a roar and broke from the circle, charging at Parker. She used War Paint's dead husk as a launching pad, stepping up and leaping over Ram. Ram's momentum skidded it into War Paint, where it croaked again as it tumbled over the carcass. Parker, having landed as gracefully as her background in gymnastics allowed under these far from professional conditions, found herself standing smackdab between Featherweight and Ol'Onesie. She winked at Ol'Onesie, just for fun, then feinted as if to grab at its remaining tusk. Her gambit fooled the beast, and it flinched away, squawking. She pivoted as Featherweight charged, and swung her leg in a roundhouse. Her heel caught Featherweight in the jaw, and it spun around in midair before careening to the ground.

Parker didn't have time to follow-up on this move because Port Wine body-checked her hip. She lost her balance in the slick snow, but faced Port Wine in time to block its thrown hooves with her forearms and deliver a jab of her own to its muddied gut. She got in a blow between its eyes before Hit N' Run (ironically?) plowed her over. It stepped on her tender abdomen, gouging a tear in her parka. She elbowed it on the ear and delivered a palm-thrust to its nose that should have knocked it off her, but its hoof tangled in the rip in her parka, and all it did was squeal and thrash. Parker rolled, narrowly avoiding another set of hooves that clomped down where her head had been. She lifted the coat over her head and squirmed out of it. In a smooth move, she slid on her knees behind Hit N'Run, its hoof still caught, and wrapped the outerwear around its face, locking its legs against it. Holding tight onto the coat with one hand, she unleashed a flurry of punches against Hit N' Run's spine until she felt multiple vertebrae snap. She chucked its paralyzed body at Port Wine as it took another run at her, and both hogs fell to the ground.

Ol'Onesie and Featherweight teamed up to charge at her from two sides. She dodged and weaved, trying to give herself more space to work with. Smush Face got a bite on her booted ankle and she swung her opposite leg, dislodging it with a shin to the neck. In a synchronized attack, Jowly threw its weight against her knee, and Ram catapulted into her chest, knocked the breath from her lungs and her feet from underneath her.

All at once, Parker realized her mistake. She'd been thinking of the feral hogs as a pack of wolves, hunting as a family but not necessarily coordinated, not with any kind of actionable plan. But that was wrong; the hogs weren't wolves, they were orcas. And Parker was a seal pup, adrift on an ice floe, just waiting to be destroyed by their next calculated assault.

"Eriksen!"

Sylvie's cry focused Parker. She scrambled up, tossing out fists, elbows and knees with abandon as she swiveled to get a look at Sylvie. She was hanging from the lowest branch now, maybe only twenty feet above the ground. Port Wine and Ol'Onesie had changed tactics, or were following a new directive, kicking and headbutting the tree trunk, trying to knock Sylvie loose while the others distracted Parker.

It wouldn't work. Parker wasn't a seal pup. The feral hogs weren't orcas or wolves or anything more than the spawn of escaped, domesticated sows and imported European wild boar. Parker wasn't a man, or a Viking goddess, or even, in this moment, a disgraced MMA fighter, descended from Norwegian royalty, and heiress to a capitalist fortune. She was a goddamn woman, and she was going to save Sylvie fucking Cahwee.

Parker's battle cry arced out of her throat like a warning bell. Her blood pulsed with renewed fervor, and she erupted at the nearest feral hog –

Smush Face – raining Shame and Loathing down on his bleating snout until all of the bones in her fingers and hands felt broken. Port Wine bit into her thigh, and she shoved him off her, grabbing his ears and pushing her face into his neck. She opened wide and bit him back, whipping her head back and forth as violently as a cat with a mouse. He tasted of dirt and shit, gamey meat and copper blood. She tore a chunk free and shoved, spitting his own honk of flesh into his eyes. Holding him by the fur of his crown, she kneed him in the snout until his tusks shattered.

At this point, Ol'Onesie and Ram had no choice but to abandon their assault on the tree and regroup. As Parker stood, huffing and puffing and dripping blood from her jaws, the four remaining feral hogs – Featherweight, Jowly, Ol'Onesie and Ram – lined up side by side, creating a wall between herself and Sylvie's tree. Their saliva had frozen against their maws, or dried up from fright. Their dark eyes tracked Parker's every move as she rolled her neck, bent her knees, and beckoned to the beasts.

"Bring it on, motherfuckers!" Parker shouted.

It was all the invitation they needed.

They charged as one, no break between their flanks, their strides even and their eyes daring her to stand her ground. She yelled and charged forward herself. At the last moment, she made as if to leap over them, and they matched her with leaps of their own. She dropped and slid under them like a baseball player stealing third. She bulleted back to her feet and tackled Jowly from behind. Grasping the hog by its tusks, she pulled it to the nearest tree, kneeing it in the ribs as it struggled. She slammed its head against the tree trunk until they were both covered with fallen snow – a matching pair except the hog was dead and Parker radiantly alive.

She faced her final three attackers. Final two. Where was Ram?

Visions of velociraptors with nine-inch hooked claws danced through Parker's mind as a low grunt rumbled over the snow behind her. She swept her gaze toward it but didn't want to lose sight of the other two. She caught its shadow, hunched, tensed – ready. The corner of Parker's lip curled into a wry smile.

"Clever gir–" But before she could finish, Hit N' Run burst out of the forest's ground cover and collided with Parker's ribs. Her spine-breaking jabs hadn't killed the thing after all, or even paralyzed it.

Hit N' Run's bulk pinned Parker to the ground on her side, one shoulder trapped between the earth and her body, her hip grinding into the torn-up forest floor. Bloody froth spurted from its rabid mouth as the hog snarled and chomped, trying to take a chunk out of Parker's face or neck. She held it at bay with her free arm, elbow sunk into the soft spot where its chin met its neck, her wrist bent painfully to allow her injured fist to grasp its ear. Its hind legs didn't kick as frantically as normal, but its forehooves packed a wallop, striking into Parker's back and chest at interchanging intervals.

"Over here!"

Parker heard Sylvie shout, and had to assume the naked, unarmed and un-professionally-trained idiot had hopped down from the relative safety of the red pine to try to lure the hogs away from Parker's prone body. Parker would have commanded her to climb her dumbass back up the tree, but when she opened her mouth, visceral muck splooged out of Hit N'Run's flared nostrils directly onto her tongue. She gagged and choked, a sound that seemed to startle the hog, because it let up a fraction. A fraction was all Parker needed to get her trapped arm out from under her side, and press her thumb into its glassy eye until it popped.

The hog howled and fell back. Parker rolled on top and added her second thumb to its other eye. She pressed both thumbs into both eyes, globs of bloody gunk spurting up her wrists. She felt slick bone, and the hog's body twitched in death throes, but Parker didn't let up. She spit its own goop back into Hit N' Run's face, laughed wildly, and looked up to see if her ruthless counterattack had gotten the other hogs' attention.

She saw Sylvie recreating the image Parker had conjured for herself only moments ago: she was the lost seal pup, precariously perched on the melting ice floe, played by the Ski-Doo. The orcas circled her, ramming the snowmobile just enough to wobble her knees and elicit a yelp, toying with her. They grunted back and forth, playfully headbutting each other in lieu of high-fives.

Parker dislodged her thumbs from Hit N' Run's eye cavities and charged. The hogs snapped into formation. Ram and Ol' Onesie faced her onslaught, while Featherweight backed up a step and hunched, preparing to taking a running leap at Sylvie. There was no way Parker could get around these two in time to block Featherweight's attack. Her heart ricocheted in her chest, the blood in her veins burning anew.

"No!" she shouted as Featherweight's hooves took to the air.

Something flew from the opposite direction, slashing across Featherweight's face and dropping him to the ground with a yip. At the same time, Parker reached the hogs' defensive line, spun left and landed a backwards kick against Ol'Onesie's ear. The hog fell against Ram, tripping them both up, landing both their snouts in the dirty snow. Parker spared a glance back toward the scene at the snowmobile.

Davey, resplendent in his tactical vest, was back on his feet. Featherweight, stunned from the in-air collision, had blood weeping from the gash across its snout. It was also somehow terrified of Davey, tripping over itself to avoid getting nipped, looking like an elephant dancing away from a mouse. Parker smiled.

That smile quickly turned into a gritted sneer as she refocused on the task at hand. Ram regained its feet, but Ol'Onesie still scrambled to find purchase in the wet and torn up ground. So she brought a knee into her chest and threw her leg down, crashing her heel into the ankle joint of Ol'Onesie's hind leg. It did the trick; the leg snapped, the hog yowled, and it was out of play for at least a few minutes.

Which was good, because Ram charged at Parker's flank. She caught its tusks with enough leverage to keep its head from slamming into her chest, but its momentum pushed her over. As she fell, she kicked up and lifted her hips, rolling them both into a half-grounded backflip. She landed on top of Ram, dug her knees into the vulnerable space where the hog's hips met its thighs to keep it in place, and jerked its head up by the tusks. She rammed its head back onto the ground until its eyes rolled up, then released a tusk to draw back her fist and throw punches at its maw until its body stopped twitching. Parker couldn't feel either of her hands anymore, but she also couldn't feel the throbbing of Ram's pulse against her legs as she straddled its chest, and that was the more important thing.

Leaving Ram's carcass to cool, she stalked toward Ol'Onesie, whose body spasmed as it dragged its leg uselessly behind it. Hot air puffed out of its nostrils as it breathed heavily, its broken tusk glinting. It stopped and stared at Parker, its midnight eyes dimmed to dusk. Its shoulders seemed to slump. It had no fight left.

Empathy socked Parker in the gut. She grunted. "Get out of here." She shooed at Ol'Onesie with her shattered hand. It huffed back at her, pivoted on its three good legs, and retreated into the cover of the forest.

At the snowmobile, Davey still had Featherweight's nonplussed attention, keeping it engaged in a two-step that had its back to Parker. She moved up on it slowly, grasped it firmly by its nose and one ear, and twisted her arms in opposite directions, snapping Featherweight's neck. Its body slumped to the ground. Davey hopped, barked, and wagged his mighty tail.

"Good dog," Parker told him.

"Holy fuck," Sylvie breathed. She still stood on the snowmobile's seat, arms wrapped around her shivering torso. She looked at Parker in a way she hadn't done before, certainly in a way Parker did not care to analyze right now.

Parker helped Sylvie down, her skin an icicle, and got her clothed in the extra gear she'd brought along. She gave Sylvie Mountain Seeker's ill-fitting fleece-lined jeans as well, opting to suffer the embarrassment of being seen in her graying long johns. She also gave Sylvie her boots, which were too big but would warm her enough to save her toes from frostbite. Parker still had her thick winter mid-calf socks, and besides, her blood was pumping far too hot through her body. Soon, the adrenaline would ebb and the pain would swell, and the cold would still be the least of her concerns.

After stowing a jubilant Davey in the emptied saddlebag, Parker mounted the snowmobile in front of Sylvie. She went ahead and let herself blush at the press of Sylvie's body against her own; her face was flush anyway with the heat of battle. Sylvie wrapped her arms around Parker. Her hands, which couldn't reach each other, gripped the fabric of Parker's flannel above her waistline. Parker sighed. They were going to be okay.

From the tree-line, Ol'Onesie hobbled into the clearing their scuffle had created. A laugh caught in Parker's throat. She thought this hog was brave, if stupid, and she'd simply run him over with the snowmobile and redub him Hit N' Run Two. But then a row of fresh, uninjured, and spitting mad feral hogs stepped into the clearing behind it. Parker could hear the groans and moans of more of the hogs' gang clomping through the forest toward them as well.

She narrowed her eyes at Ol'Onesie. "I thought we struck an accord, you little fucker."

"What?" Sylvie asked.

"I said we're fucked."

Davey started barking in his saddlebag. The crush of feral hogs backed up a pace, looking a bit jittery.

"Get us the fuck out of here, Eriksen!"

Parker floored it.

The snowmobile spun out of the clearing, kicking up a semi-circle of snow and grit that smacked into the swarm of hogs. The Ski-Doo raced through the trees, careening toward the valley. The wind ripped Davey's barks from his yap faster than he could launch them and Parker zigged around a copse of firs, catching sight of the pack of hogs out of the corner of her eye. They were chasing the snowmobile, plowing through the snow, banking off of tree trunks, trampling over each other to reach their prey. Parker gunned the engine, relishing the black smoke that exploded out of the exhaust. The hogs receded from view, and the valley materialized beyond the trees up ahead.

"Yipee kiyah, motherfuckers!" Parker pounded a triumphant fist into the air.

The snowmobile lurched to a stop, pitching Parker's pelvis into the handlebars. Sylvie's anxious grip tightened around Parker's abdomen. Davey followed the sudden stop's momentum and hopped out of the saddle bag, and lifted his leg to write his name in the snow. The blinking red light on the snowmobile's dash all but exploded.

Out of gas.

Sylvie's palm beat frantically against Parker's back. "What are you doing? Go, go, go!"

"I can't, we're stalled out, we gotta...." Hooves crunched through snow. Dark bodies crashed through underbrush. Murderous snorts boomeranged through the hollow forest. Parker gulped. "We gotta run."

"Run?" Sylvie sounded incredulous, but there was nothing for it.

Parker swept her leg over the snowmobile, gently gliding Sylvie off the seat as well. She scooped Davey up and made a break for it, barreling toward the tree-line and the open air of the valley. They couldn't outrun feral hogs. Those beasts could max out at thirty miles per hour, humans only about fifteen, and that assumed no injuries, no exhaustion, no fifteen-pound yapping dog in your arms. Parker considered tossing Davey like a grenade into the midst of the encroaching onslaught, but thought better of it; Featherweight's bewildered fear of the tiny terrier may have been a fluke, and even if it wasn't, the hogs had numbers on their side—they'd trample poor Davey eventually. She couldn't sacrifice him like that, just to buy her and Sylvie a couple minutes to escape across the valley. But—

As the valley opened up, and the hoofbeats and squealing closed in behind them, an idea sparked through Parker's heated mind. She fumbled with a zipper on Davey's tactical vest, slowing down in the process. Sylvie turned back, waving her arms wildly. "Come on, come on, Eriksen! I'm not dying at my fucking place of employment!"

"Hang on, almost...almost..." Parker got the zipper down, pulled her cell phone out of the pocket and thumbed it on. She swiped through screens to find the right app, then scrolled with a confident focus she didn't actually feel, Sylvie shouting at her and then tugging on her, the hot, eggy breath of thirty to fifty feral hogs all but puffing down her neck as she watched the file-loading bar inch home.

Finally, the track completed its download. Parker spun on her heel, tried not to cry out at the many beastly faces she encountered, so close now she could see the killing fervor in their beady eyes. She amped the volume up on her phone, held it aloft, and pressed play.

The roar of helicopter blades sliced through the crisp air. The feral hogs skidded to a halt, bumping into each other and taking nosedives into the snow. Their collective growls and snorts of slavering hunters abruptly morphed into the warning cries and squeals of prey on-the-run. They retreated, their brown bottoms bobbing almost cutely back into the cover of the trees.

"I can't believe that worked!" Parker exclaimed.

"You're a genius," Sylvie said dryly. She tugged on Parker's sleeve. "Now let's go!"

Parker set Davey down, and the three sprinted through the valley to the village gate. Parker held the phone out the whole way, sometimes running backwards to make sure the feral hogs weren't following. The sound of the helicopter triggered their flight response and kept them at bay, but they lingered, hooting and bleating at the tree line. At the gate, Parker left her phone on the post; she didn't know if the hogs would actually penetrate the village proper in order to hunt them down, but after what Ol'Onesie pulled, she wasn't taking any chances.

The three of them were safe. For now.

Chapter Six

Back at her apartment, Parker ran Sylvie a warm bath and left her to recover in privacy. She hooked Davey up with a ham sandwich and bowl of water, draping his tactical vest over the back of her chair like a hero veterans flight jacket. Then she peeled off her own clothes, careful around the most egregious injuries. She hadn't realized how caked with gore and dirt everything had gotten, especially the skin of her face, neck, hands and arms. Her hair was a goner; she might as well shave it off than try to detangle the gunky mess it had become. Lacking clippers, she did her best to clean herself up in the half bathroom, scrubbing and wiping until she was too tired to do anymore. She took the most relieving pee of her life, and stepped back into her room.

Sylvie was in her bed. She'd tied her hair up in a towel, slipped into one of Parker's oversized sweatshirts, and snuggled under a fresh duvet she must have pulled out of Parker's closet, Davey asleep in her lap. She sipped from a large bottle of water and nibbled at her own ham sandwich, rubbing a serene Davey behind his ears, looking for all the world like she was enjoying a comfy Sunday morning in bed. Except for the puckered gash across her brow, the myriad scratches on her hands and cheeks, the chunk that had been taken out of her right earlobe, and the shockingly purple bruise that stretched across her collarbone, disappearing beneath the neckline of the sweatshirt.

Parker swiped a towel off a hook in the bathroom before Sylvie looked her way. She didn't wrap it around herself fast enough (and it didn't fit completely around her bulk anyway, exposing her entire side up to her chest), and Sylvie couldn't contain her gasp. "My god, Eriksen, you look like hell."

Parker smirked. "The Viking goddess, or the final resting place?"

Sylvie lifted the covers next to her. "Get in here and let me tend to you."

Blood rushed to Parker's groin. She blinked and walked away from the bed, to her dresser instead. "I've suffered worse," she offered. She bent to open her dresser drawer and hitched up, wincing at the shooting pain in her abdomen. Maybe she could nudge the drawer open by wedging her knee under the handle....

A warm hand caressed her back, and Sylvie guided her out of the way. She opened her drawers, selected a pair of sweats and a t-shirt. "Don't be so stubborn," Sylvie said. "Or modest. Give me that towel."

Part of Parker was ecstatic to hand the reins over to Sylvie; she'd been steering this boat of survival since the night of the hunt, and she was beyond exhausted. What could it hurt to let someone else take the rudder for the few minutes it took to get dressed? Let Sylvie make the choices Parker was tired of bumbling. On the other hand, she hadn't let anyone steer her into anything since Ray and her family crashed her into the iceberg of MMA fraud and illegal gambling. Even if she was relatively safe letting Sylvie lead her through the motions of getting dressed, maybe applying a bandage or two, it wasn't anything like what Ray and her father had done. How much damage could Sylvie really do to her in only a few minutes? Then again, wasn't that exactly the question Parker had asked Coach Vic? It's just a lunch meeting, Coach. What could it hurt?

The callouses of Sylvie's palms brushed Parker's swollen cheeks. She blinked back into the here and now, into the warm room and the hot woman cupping her face in her hands.

"Parker." Her voice was too sweet, her eyes like an inviting sea. She'd never called Parker by her first name; it was always Eriksen, even when they'd spent that drunken night together. Hearing it on Sylvie's tongue made Parker's ears steam. "I see that ridiculous brain of yours working overtime, puzzling out how this could all go wrong. But listen to me—everything is upside down, okay? This, right here, in your room, now? This is as safe and normal as anything is ever going to get. Just—stop thinking, stop second-guessing, stop trying to predict. Just listen to me and give me the towel."

Her words soothed Parker like a salve. She did as she was told. Sylvie helped her step into the sweatpants, and then pull the t-shirt over her head. It was slow going; Parker's muscles were sore and stiff, her bones creaky and weak. When she was dressed, Sylvie made her sit on the edge of the bed (Davey curled up against her back, soothing her even more with the soft beating of his little dog heart), and retrieved the first aid kit from a cabinet in the shared bathroom. She cracked open the two ice packs and laid them atop Parker's bashed knuckles, then she rubbed her hands over a hot pack, the friction heating it up, and pressed it gently over Parker's tender kidney. Finally, she got a stack of bandages and anti-bacterial cream together, and started applying both to the various shallow lacerations across Parker's arms, chest, neck, torso and face.

"Jesus," Sylvie whistled through her teeth while she worked. "I can't tell which of these you got fighting at Jimmy's and which you got today."

"Or during the hunt," Parker reminded her.

"Yeah, the hunt." Sylvie shook her head a bit. Parker allowed herself one quick sniff of Sylvie's hair: plums and daffodils. "You know, the guys told me what you do out there, during those hunts. How you beat the shit of all those hogs with your bare hands. I believed them, but truthfully? I couldn't picture it. It just sounded so...ruthless."

Sylvie tore open an alcohol pad and wiped at a particularly gnarly cut over Parker's ribs. Parker winced, more at Sylvie's words than at the sting of the alcohol. "Those fights are supposed to be private."

"I can understand why." Sylvie was silent for a moment, then: "When I watch you at Jimmy's, it's like you're just, I don't know, doing a job. Getting it done for the paycheck. Punching by rote. There's no...no life in it, you know? No life in you. But today, Eriksen, out there, what I saw you do? The way you did it. The look in your eyes? Eriksen, you weren't just alive. You were..." Her eyes slid away from Parker's as she thought, and then slid back. "You were feral."

At her words, something other than internal bleeding broke free inside Parker's gut. Disgust. Maybe pride.

Sylvie returned her gaze to her work. "Is that how you were back in the day, in the MMA ring? If so, I can see why you were a champion."

Parker blew bitter air between her clenched teeth. "That wasn't my ferocity, that was my father's money."

"Bullshit." Sylvie didn't hesitate, shaking her head a fraction. "Everyone knows you're a fighter, a real fighter. That's why so many of these hothead men want to take you on at Jimmy's. You're an actual challenge, and they want the clout that comes with beating a true athlete, you know, not just some bulked-up chick but a skilled bulked-up chick." She laughed dryly. "You should hear some of the praise you get after fights. You would hear it, if you hung around, or came down to the bar, mingled a little."

Parker felt her ears redden as her mind flashed on memories of the last time she "mingled" with Sylvie. She looked away, timed her breathing to the rhythm of Davey's chest falls against her back. "I don't fight at Jimmy's for the accolades, Sylvie."

"Why do you fight, then?"

"Preparation." Parker's voice hitched; she cleared her throat. She was forced to look at Sylvie as the woman placed her fingertips beneath Parker's chin and turned her face to look at her. She patted an alcohol swab along the slash above Parker's brow, the cut she received at Jimmy's that had reopened during her battle today. "For the hunt. For...So I don't get the shit completely beat out of me while I do something wildly stupid. I don't want to die, or get so hurt I can't recover in a week, minimum. I just want to...I don't know..." She spread her hands, looked fixedly at her palms.

"Feel something?" Sylvie ventured.

"Repent," Parker said at the same time.

They locked eyes. Parker tasted the memory of Sylvie's lips on hers, her tongue in her mouth, burning with want. Slowly, she traced her thumb across the laceration above Sylvie's brow. She smirked, "Twins."

Sylvie reached up and brought Parker's raw and broken hand down to rest between her own palms. "I'd rather not think of us as related."

A bubble of laughter popped out of Parker like a hiccup. She blinked and broke Sylvie's gaze. Sylvie rummaged through the first aid kit again, pulling out gauze, Bactine, and more bandages, and started tending to Parker's hands. They were numb, and Parker stretched her back, looking out of the window beyond Sylvie as she worked in silence. Snow was starting to fall again in great whirls, the wind picking up, buffeting the frosted windowpane. She had no idea what time it was, but the sky was dark with thick, gray clouds. The smell of burnt hair seeped into the room as the radiator rasped out its heat.

When Sylvie broke the silence, Parker's spine tensed, startled out of her blissfully blank meditation. "That one hog, the one that almost got me? He was scared of Davey, don't you think? It was...strange. And I mean, considering the epic strangeness of all of this, that's saying something."

"Yeah," agreed Parker. "I don't think Davey's ever even seen a feral hog. But he was a bait dog, so he's used to going up against larger foes."

"That doesn't explain why the hog was so skittish."

Parker shrugged. "Why are we so scared of spiders? Or rats."

Sylvie huffed a laugh, assenting.

"Actually, have you ever heard the story of the hooyups?"

Sylvie quirked a questioning eyebrow.

"It's a child's bedtime story. Maybe specific to Norway, I don't know."

"Wait." Sylvie packed up the first aid kit and laid it back on the dresser. She tore open a couple foil packets of ibuprofen, handed a few caplets to Parker along with a bottle of water, and they toasted each other as they downed the medicine. Then Sylvie crawled back into Parker's bed, getting cozy under the covers. She pulled the blanket back for Parker, patted the pillow next to her. "Get in, and tell me this bedtime story."

Parker disguised her hesitation by fussing over Davey for a moment, fluffing the blankets at Sylvie's feet so he could curl up there, kissing his snoot and tossing him a couple "good boys." Finally, she couldn't avoid it any longer; it would be weird if she sat in the chair after Sylvie had taken such gentle care of her wounds and invited her into the bed. She didn't want to be rude, or ungrateful, or cold. They had just been through an ordeal together, surreal as it was, and Parker still had plenty of questions of her own for Sylvie. She could get into bed with the ranger, tell her tall tale, and then get the answers she needed. It didn't have to be anything else. It wouldn't be.

Parker settled in beside Sylvie, pulling the duvet all the way up to her neck. Sensing her discomfort, Sylvie rolled onto her back and closed her eyes. She sighed deeply. "All right, Eriksen. Tell me about these Q-tips."

"Hooyups." Parker corrected. "My au pair told it to me as if it happened to her. She said when she was small, her family had a vacation home on the lake, a cabin they shared with her grandparents. One summer, they found a little dog begging for scraps on their doorstep. He was butt ugly, all scraggly and dirty, but she, the au pair, fell instantly in love. Neither her parents nor her grandparents could convince her to let the dog go. So, it was her dog, and she named him Turly because he looked like a curly turd."

Sylvie snorted laughter.

Parker smiled and went on. "He was generally a good dog, but at night he would bark like wild, running from window to window. My au pair's father got fed up with it, and locked Turly in the broom closet one night. Unbeknownst to the family, however, Turly wasn't just barking at nothing; as soon as the moon reached the acme of the sky, the hooyups emerged from their underground lair and stalked out to the cabin. They were called hooyups because that's the sound they made as they surrounded their prey, closing in for the kill. Hooyup! Hooyup! Hooyup!"

At the foot of the bed, Davey's ears twitched. Sylvie rubbed his rump with her foot through the blanket.

"The hooyups ran around the cabin, crying 'hooyup, hooyup!' In the closet, little Turly scratched at the door, barking and snarling. But the closet contained his noise, so no one woke up when the hooyups busted down the cabin door and stole into the parent's bedroom. They carried off Papa and Mama, and were about to enter the grandparents' room, when Turly finally broke down the closet door and barked and barked and barked, chasing the hooyups back into their underground lair. When my au pair and her grandparents woke up, they blamed Turly for the mess, and figured Papa and Mama had left to find Turly's owner, to send him back because he was such a menace.

"The next night, grandpa locked Turly in the bathroom. But as soon as the moon shone high in the sky, the hooyups returned. They circled the cabin once more, crying 'hooyup, hooyup, hooyup!'"

This time, Sylvie joined in on making the hooyup sounds, and the two women giggled together. Parker stole a glance at Sylvie, her eyes still closed but her mouth grinning wide. Parker let her knee stray to rest against Sylvie's leg. She noted the blush that darkened Sylvie's perfect cheek, averted her eyes back to the ceiling, and continued:

"In the bathroom, little Turly was barking and snarling and throwing his tiny body at the door. The hooyups broke into the cabin again, rushed into the grandparents' room, and carried grandpa and grandma off to their lair. Just as they were about to barge into the au pair's room, Turly broke the bathroom door off its hinges and chased the hooyups away, back to their underground lair.

"In the morning, when my au pair couldn't find grandma or grandpa, she followed Turly's tracks and found him sniffing at a hole in the ground near the lake's shore. Turly barked and barked, and growled and growled, and my au pair went back to the cabin to grab a shovel. They dug together at the hole until they unearthed the entryway to the hooyups' lair. Terrified of little Turly, the hooyups retreated deeper and deeper into their cavern, finally offering up grandpa, grandma, Mama and Papa to my au pair, if she would only take Turly away. Reunited, the family returned to their cabin. That night, they left Turly out in the living room, and when the hooyups came jumping around, Turly barked and barked, chasing them away. And the family, knowing now that they were protected, were calmed by Turly's barking, and slept through 'til morning.

"Now, of course, that lake has dried up, and they've built a subdivision there. But it's said, when the moon rises high in the sky, if you bend your ear to the street, you can still hear them deep in their underground lair. Hooyup! Hooyup! Hooyup!"

Sylvie clapped her hands, laughing. "A beautiful tale. Kind of morbid for a kid's story, though."

"Well, no one gets eaten," Parker countered. "Not like Little Red Riding Hood."

"True enough."

Another silence settled between them. Davey began to snore. Parker felt the tension in her muscles relax, her bones loosen. She closed her eyes, but the darkness troubled her. Before she could stop herself, she reached over and grasped Sylvie's hand. The ranger trembled but her grip was firm. When Parker looked, she saw that Sylvie was crying.

"Sylvie," she tried to make her voice sound gentle, reassuring, but there was a tremor of fear in it, of knowing, if Sylvie answered her question, the story she had to tell would not be a kind one. "What happened to you? What happened to everyone?"

"We got hooyupped," Sylvie said. Her fingers tightened around Parker's. Parker held in her wince. "I was at the bar, ordering another round for the boys, when people started shouting. Screaming, more like. A few rifle shots popped off, and then folks started running pell-mell. I slipped on someone's spilled beer, cracked my skull against a table." She raised her eyebrows, indicating the gash there. "I feel like...like the rest of it was a dream. A nightmare. It didn't make any sense. Still doesn't."

Parker allowed her a rattling intake of breath, then caressed the backs of her knuckles with the calloused pad of her thumb. Sylvie exhaled into a resigned sigh.

"I came in and out," she continued. "I remember opening my eyes to snow caking my lashes. Everything was blurry. I was being pushed, or pulled, on what felt like a sled, maybe a cart but the ride was smooth, like on skis, not a wheel. I could feel this...this presence behind me, and in front of me, and all around me. These hulking forms. Heard them too, grunting and smacking their lips. And the smell—god, the smell ripened as we went on, felt like we were getting closer and closer to a trash heap, or a compost pile. I figured I'd hit my head just a mite too hard, went and got myself killed in the dumbest way possible, and now here were these devils, dragging my dumbass to hell. Well, I wasn't too far off, really.

"I blinked out again, came to again, on and on like that for who knows how long. Always, that smell got stronger, the ride became bumpier; I slid all over the place, back and forth, but I was strapped in tight, and now there was blood in my eye, from the gash. I think I tried to speak, to ask what the hell was going on, to beg the devils to release me, give me a chance, you know? Give me a chance to make it up, whatever I'd done to be brought here. But I was frozen up, I guess, couldn't make my mouth open, or my throat do much more than swallow. And it got hotter, and I stopped struggling to stay awake, because if I was going in the blaze, I didn't want to be conscious for it.

"The next time I woke up, I was upright, sitting against a hot rock that scalded my back. I scuttled away and got my bearings. It was too dark to see anything, but I heard water dripping somewhere, and I felt the rocks around me and below me. I crawled around; it was too narrow for me to stand. Cave wasn't much larger than a coffin, and I was naked, and sore, and I smelled dirt and shit, and I started thinking it was a coffin. I don't know how long I was in that place, Eriksen. Felt like ages. I pounded on the walls, got myself all twisted up so I didn't know which way was which. I found the little stream of water made by the drips down the sides of the rock, lapped it up like a dog, like a goddamn animal. It was warm, like piss, and it only made my belly ache for something more substantial.

"Eventually, they came for me. The rock rolled back and light shined it, nearly blinded me. I squinted against it and a reeking bulbous shadow lumbered into the cave, gripped my ankle in its slobbering maw, and dragged me out. I didn't even scream, and if I did, it was to say thank you. Thank you for getting me out of that grave. When my eyes adjusted, I saw I was in this massive cavern, lit by torches and fire pits. There were caves like mine scattered up the walls, disappearing into the darkness beyond the stalactites. Stairs had been etched into the cavern, and a rail system ran through the space, tunneled into the walls and came back out a level or two up. I was on the bottom level, surrounded by feral hogs, all in various stages of dragging my naked neighbors out of their catacombs."

Parker tried to picture the scene, and came up with the Orc mines in Lord of the Rings, except in place of their fantastical, toothy faces, she conjured Ol'Onesie, its tusks gloriously intact, glowering at its prisoners.

"Even with everything you just did, Eriksen," Sylvie said, looking at her and then looking just as quickly away. "I'm afraid you won't believe me. I barely believe me. It was...unreal. The hogs, they were standing on their hind legs, most of them, and they kicked tools at us—shovels, pickaxes, hammers. They grunted as if they were trying to speak to us, and performed, like, charades to indicate what they wanted us to do. Sam Delgado, you know how pigheaded he can be, he rushed at one of the hogs, tried to take him down at the knee. You fought that idiot in the ring, you know he's a shit fighter, and thinks he's brawnier than he is. The only swollen muscle he has is his ego. Of course, he was swarmed and hooved to a pulp. They rolled him back into his little cave and didn't drag him back out for hours.

"After that, no one else tried anything. Patty, poor woman, caught my eye and tried to say something to me, and got nipped in the calf for her trouble. One by one, we picked up our tools and went where we thought the hogs wanted us to go. There were these stalagmites, or what I guess could be called stalagmites, piercing out of the ground all over the place. In some spots, they shimmered, and that's where we aimed our tools. It was a lot of effort, hacking and slashing at those damn shimmers, until we unearthed these gleaming ice blue gems about the size of a marble. When we finally chipped one out, we chucked it into the carts that the hogs pushed along the tracks, collecting everyone's gems.

"I don't know how long this went on. Everything was dark, and stank, and it was so hot, and there were no breaks, just banging and banging and banging away. I couldn't feel my arms after a while; my fingers wouldn't grip right. I got a couple beatings for dropping my axe. After a time, one of the hogs bleated out, and we were returned to our caves. I almost fought back at that point; as terrible as the labor was, I didn't want to go back in there. But then I remembered there was water, and I went willingly.

"I guess I slept, and then it started all over again. I—wait, how long has it been?"

"Since the night of the hogs? Two and a half days, about."

"That's it? Christ, it felt like so much longer. I lost count of how many rotations we did, how many beatings, how many ice blue gems were collected and carted off. But I felt myself weakening with each cycle, and I knew if any of us was going to get out of here, we had to do it before our strength was completely sapped. I didn't see everyone from the village in my part of the cavern, but I saw enough folks to deduce the entirety of Hekla Lake must be there, and those unlucky visitors, like myself, who'd been in town when the feral hogs raided. I thought about you, Eriksen, but I couldn't imagine you being bossed around by these beasts. It was too much to hope that you'd somehow escaped and would send help back for us. I knew I had to get out, get back to the village and call for help, or at least to the ranger station or one of the towers for the radio.

"So, back in my cell, I lapped up as much water as I could stomach, tried to sleep a bit, so I'd be as rested as possible for my grand escape. In reality, it wasn't really grand. There was no way for me to signal any of the other villagers to create a distraction for me, not even Patty, who threw me pitiful looks as she chipped away at her own stalagmite a level above me. All I had going for me was the pickaxe in my aching arms, and the element of surprise. On a random swing, I pivoted and struck my overseer across the maw with the blunt side of the axe, and I ran. I followed the cart tracks into the tunnel, burying the business end of the axe in the hairy ear of one of my pursuers. There were torches in the tunnel, spaced like markers along the wall. I just kept running, ignoring the wet, huffing breaths behind me, and pounding hooves. I ran until I saw light, and then I ran harder.

"I came out into the forest, into the snow, and it slowed me down. But I kept pushing; the cold was welcome after all that heat, but it froze my sweat to my skin, and it numbed my feet, causing me to stumble. I heard the feral hogs gaining on me. I knew I couldn't make it very far. I climbed the first tree that had low enough branches for me to leap onto. I used the last of my strength to get as high as I could; maybe the hogs would race right under me, pass me by and keep on going. No such luck. I thought I was dead. For real dead this time. The look in their eyes as they circled below me, like sharks, like piranhas. I was gonna be eaten alive, and those bastards would start with my toes, make sure I felt every chomp until they reached my vital organs. So, I screamed, the scream of a dying woman, of a life cut short. But then—you saved me."

Their eyes locked. Sylvie turned, propping her head up with one hand, her other moving to trace fingertips across the inside of Parker's elbow. "Thank you, Parker."

Parker imagined the suffocating heat of the feral hogs' cavern couldn't hold a candle to the blaze burning through her from Sylvie's unbroken gaze. Her pulse quickened, and she was sure Sylvie could feel it in the veins in her arm. She realized she hadn't said anything in far too long, was just staring and sweating, but her tongue felt heavy, her mind suddenly foggy. "Um," she licked her lips. "You're welcome."

Sylvie held her eye contact for a beat longer, then blinked and retracted her fingers. The abrupt absence of warmth almost made Parker wretch ruefully, but she gracefully turned it into a cough.

"What were you doing out there, anyway?" Sylvie asked her.

Parker told her about waking up in the valley after the hunt, surrounded by snow and uncollected feral hog carcasses. She told her about the gouges she found at her apartment door, and later, the identical marks she spotted at the Mountain Seeker homestead. She tried to describe the eerie stillness of Hekla Lake the past few days, the creeping dread that forced her mind to retreat from her unsettling present into unwanted memories from her past. Finally, she told Sylvie about the blocked main road down the mountain, the boon of the snowmobile, and her plan to reach the fire tower to call the park rangers for help.

"So, I guess I should really be thanking you," she said. "For telling me about the satellite radio stored out there. I got through to someone; they said they're sending a helicopter to check on things.

Couldn't give me an ETA before I heard your SOS, but—"

Sylvie sat up, excited. "Which ranger station?"

Parker thought back. "A6, I think."

Sylvie cursed under her breath, then turned her whole body to look pensively out of the window. At her feet, Davey snorted his disapproval of the position shift, scooted his little body to a spot more in the center of the bed, away from squirming legs and feet.

"Second wave of the storm is coming in too strong," Sylvie said. She spoke to the window pane, to the wind and swirling precipitation beyond. "That station's not close. Even if they relayed the message to a closer outpost, with this storm...How long do you think that helicopter app will hold off the throng?"

"The phone's fully charged." Parker shrugged, tensing at the serious air that descended upon Sylvie like a shroud. She preferred the heat. "So maybe, twelve hours? Assuming it doesn't freeze."

Sylvie nodded, the gears in her brain turning. She got up, letting in so much cold that Parker shivered. Sylvie went to the microwave. The digital clockface flashed twelve because Parker never bothered to set it. Sylvie tapped the "timer" button and punched in eight hours.

"I know you're not going to want to hear this, but we can't wait for reinforcements. In the conditions they're under, I don't think our friends in the mine can wait much longer for rescue. We have to get them out ourselves, Eriksen. It's up to you and me."

In the movie adaptation of this chapter of their lives, this is the part where the music would swell and the heroines would look resolvedly at each other, one of them grinning as the other quipped, and the dog championed a bark as he launched himself off the bed, ready for action.

Parker slumped against the pillows of her bed and moaned. "Are you kidding me?"

Sylvie jumped back into bed, bending over Parker and taking her by the waist to shake her. The towel fell away from Sylvie's head, and her still-damp hair tickled Parker's scarred forehead. She smelled like blooming flowers, like fresh-cut grass, like a garden in Spring. The heat returned, and Parker clamped her arms to her sides to keep her own stink from wafting up out of her armpits.

"Come on, Viking Goddess," Sylvie jostled Parker. "This is your moment. I know you're beat, I know you're broken, but no one else can do this. No one else can do what you do. I'll get us to the cavern, you slaughter the keepers. You'll be a legend, Eriksen. The savior of Hekla Lake."

"I don't want to be a legend." Parker sounded much more petulant than she intended. She tried to wiggle out of Sylvie's grip, but that only made the ranger throw her legs around Parker to straddle her thighs. She leaned back, arms crossed, looking down her nose as Parker squirmed. "I didn't come here to save anyone, Sylvie. That isn't...that isn't my job. I don't want to run in there and...make a spectacle of myself. Have everyone whispering how, how feral I am. Gossiping about me, and writing news articles, and blogs, and local TV, and, and...I don't want...I don't want..."

Sylvie's palm pressed firmly against Parker's heaving chest, the weight and warmth of it instantly calming. As Parker babbled about everything she didn't want, Sylvie leaned down closer and closer. Parker didn't even notice until Sylvie's lips closed around hers, and she shut her mouth. Sylvie parted it again with her tongue, and they kissed until the rhythm of Parker's palpitating heart matched Sylvie's.

Sylvie pulled back an inch, trailing Parker's heat with her. They locked eyes, half open in lust. "Do this for me, Parker? Save them for me."

When the timer on the microwave buzzed eight hours later, the pair geared up and set out for the old Hekla mine.

Chapter Seven

Parker and Sylvie decided quickly that they wouldn't be able to enter the cavern the way Sylvie had escaped. Even if an impenetrable line of mercenary hogs hadn't been cowering in wait at the tree line across the snow-filled valley, Sylvie figured the mine shaft she'd escaped out of would either be closed off now, or even more heavily guarded. They would have to take their chances entering through the main mine shaft at the northern tip of the Village of Hekla Lake, and hope there was a clear path down to the hogs' mine.

They also decided to leave Davey behind, in the relative safety of the apartment. Although he'd saved their butts once, and the hogs were clearly trepidatious about him, Sylvie postulated it would be best to enter the mine with stealth. Parker let Davey out to do his business, made sure his food and water bowls were full and his bed was fluffed, kissed his marred snout, and said her goodbyes in private. The human body was a fragile thing; she could take beatings as severe as everything she'd suffered these past several days and heal up just fine, only to bump her head on a low-hanging beam in the mine shaft and die in two hours from a brain bleed, or step on a rusty nail and die in a week from an infection. In any case, these were strange days, and she needed Davey to know if she didn't come back, it wasn't because she'd abandoned him, like so many others had.

"Thanks for the assist back there yesterday," she whispered into his only ear. He nuzzled his apple-shaped head into her neck and whined. "I love you, buddy. Be good. I'll be back, or else I won't, but I'll try my damnedest." One more kiss to his noggin, and then she swept out of the room, making sure the door was shut and locked securely behind her. However Davey got out the night of the hunt, he might be able to do so again, but at least she could be confident – based on the splintered grooves in her door and baseboards – that an attempt by any of the feral hogs to get in would result in abject failure.

Parker only had one pair of snowshoes, and she wasn't keen on wasting time breaking into a neighbor's house to search for theirs. Sylvie donned the shoes and took point on the long trudge up Main Street to the closed-off mine entrance. She wanted Parker to reserve her energy for any hogs she might encounter in the mine. To that end, Sylvie exhausted herself ahead of Parker, packing down a path in the still-falling snow for Parker to follow.

They rested now and again, leaning against hulking clumps that had been vehicles before the snow overtook them. They refueled with water and jerky from Parker's stores, a pack of cheddar cheese slices and a couple mushy apples. During their rest breaks, they also volleyed theories about what the hogs were up to, and how they were able to carry out their seemingly dastardly plot.

"What if the blue ore is some kind of...alien technology?" Parker wondered aloud.

Sylvie tore off a mouthful of jerky, said around it, "You believe in aliens?"

Parker shrugged. "Is that really crazier than anything else that's been happening here?"

"All right," Sylvie conceded, "So it's aliens...."

"They left something behind a long time ago, and the hogs got to it. They're living in these mountains, trying to find shelter, they wander into the mines, root around as they do, and bump into this stuff. Obviously, they eat it."

"Obviously," Sylvie repeated, smirking around her jerky.

"Turns out it's like, um, like intelligence pills, basically." Sylvie's groan made Parker defensive, but she was self-aware enough to know how silly it sounded. Almost as silly as preternaturally sentient hogs who walked on two legs and used hand tools. "I don't know, I mean they got this way somehow, right? And the only thing that doesn't fit is the blue ore, like what is it, why do they want it so badly? Maybe it, I don't know, enhanced their brains and now they want to...to take revenge on us for hunting them, and use us to harvest the stuff why they're at it."

"If that's true, they should've grabbed you the other night."

Parker recalled awaking in the valley, blanketed by blood and snow. The marks on her apartment door. "I don't think they could find me."

Sylvie tossed a bottled water to Parker and they both drank. After a minute, Sylvie shook her head. "Nah, I'm thinking Skinwalkers."

Parker wiped a dribble of water from her chin before it could harden into ice. "How's that?"

"You heard of 'em? It's Native lore, not Yuchi...Navajo, I think. It's a form of spiritual transcendence. Skinwalkers are just folks, human most of the time, but they invoke an animal counterpart to change into when they need guidance or some shit."

"Like werewolves? How is that any better than aliens."

"Not werewolves, you ass," Sylvie's smirk was back. Parker could get used to it. "They can change at will, and into whatever. But some of them get attached to a particular form, and if they stay in it too long, they can get trapped. So, maybe one of these Skinwalkers lived with the hogs a bit too long, maybe more than one, got stuck in that form. Somewhere along the line they sired a new generation of hogs that had more intelligence, and, like you said, a vendetta."

"Sired?" Parker shivered. "Ew."

Sylvie shoved their plastic bottles into their packs, prepared to get moving again. "It's a theory."

"What about the ore?"

"Maybe it's worth something." She tightened the straps on the snowshoes, glanced up at Parker through her bangs. "Then again, maybe we're both wrong. Maybe they're hooyups after all."

Although Sylvie's tone grasped at playful, she didn't quite reach it. Parker thought again of the scrapes and gouges on her door, at Mountain Seeker's barn. Maybe something hadn't been trying to get inside; maybe something had been dancing.

The two said nothing further on the matter, and trudged on.

By the time they reached the boarded-up mouth of the Hekla Mine, the storm had ebbed, leaving clear, sun-lit skies and a rising fog of heat. Sylvie relinquished her role as the muscle to let Parker pry enough boards from the lip of the mine opening for them both to sidle through. Inside, it was like entering a sleep-deprivation chamber. Darkness swallowed all, including sound, and they pushed in, following cart tracks, until they lost the last of the light from the receding mine opening.

Sylvie flicked on the flashlight she'd borrowed from the pub's toolbox and led the way until the pair hit a junction. Here, the tracks split off into two directions, dipping down deeper into the belly of the mountain. Sylvie stood at the base of each in turn, listening for the sound of blunt tools slapping rock. She put her hand out to see if she could feel changes in the air from people's shifting weight, or vibrations from the hogs' grunting commands.

She rejoined Parker at the center of the junction, where she was rummaging through the duffel bag that held their rations and equipment. "I'm gonna take an educated guess and say it's the left path," Sylvie said, indicating the tunnel with a wave of the flashlight. "I can't hear anything, but the air feels slightly warmer, like maybe some torches are burning down that way."

"I trust you," Parker said, and found she meant it outside the breadth of this moment. Not only because they'd been physically intimate in a passionate way Parker didn't even realize was possible until she'd met Sylvie, but because Sylvie's eyes, Parker was quickly learning, didn't lie. It might have been the woman's only flaw, if you could term it that. She trained those emerald greens on Parker, and the words she spoke couldn't help but come out honest. She didn't make promises, she made statements, undisputable and solid as stone.

"I could go down the right, you take the left," Sylvie went on. "If we don't find anything within, say, five minutes, we hike back up here and regroup. Or, I guess, if I hike back up here and you're not here, I head down your direction and meet you."

"No." Parker pulled a sharp kitchen knife out of the duffel, carefully sheathed it in the beltloop of her jeans. She grabbed a hammer, pilfered from the pub's same toolbox, secured it in the opposite beltloop, and took out the duct tape and two-inch drywall nails. "I'll go down the tunnel alone. You need to stay up here, to help the villagers out as I send them up." She started taping up her wrists and knuckles, placing a nail pointed-tip out between each knuckle, so when she threw a fist at the next hog, the nails would puncture its thick hide, and hopefully stay lodged in there when she retracted her arm. If they didn't, she'd simply punch again.

"Remind me, Sylvie," Parker looked up from her work. "Why aren't we going in there with rifles again?"

"When's the last time you shot a rifle, or any gun?" Sylvie didn't need to wait for Parker's answer. "You're as likely to shoot a friendly, or your damn self, as you are a hog, whether directly or by ricochet."

"Right, so I'm going in stealthy," she went on. Sylvie knelt beside her, helped her wrap up her right hand with the tape and nails when she finished with the left. "I'll send as many villagers out as I can, one by one, and you get them to the street. I'll take out as many hogs as I can, too, before my presence triggers a melee. I don't want to get caught down there, not enough room to maneuver. If I get overwhelmed, I'll come running. You hear the sound of thirty to fifty little feral hog hooves beating it up this tunnel? That's your cue to start running, too."

Sylvie scoffed. "Thirty to fifty? More like a hundred to one-fifty."

The last thing Parker pulled out of the duffel was a coil of nylon rope. She looped this to her belt too and stood up. "Whatever the number, I'll take them down. It's what I do."

Sylvie rose with Parker, cupped her face in her hands. "No," she said. Her eyes darkened in the flashlight beam. "It's who you are."

She kissed Parker. They shared one last lustful gaze before Sylvie turned away to prepare "welcome back from the hog mines" kits for the rescued villagers: a bottle of water, a pack of tuna, and an orange for each person (or the first twenty, at least, like a weird door prize). Parker headed down the left tunnel, no flashlight for fear of giving away her approach. She thought she felt the air in the tunnel warm up by one or two degrees and knew in her gut Sylvie had chosen correctly.

Parker moved slowly, as lightly as her frame, her winter clothes, and her equipment would allow. She felt every chipped and splintered bone in her body sliding around by nanometers; heard every miniscule scrape or bandaged-up wound sucking against her bruising skin as she walked. Her mind raced through her previous altercations with the feral hogs like a flipbook: a punch thrown connecting to a tusked maw; a planted foot stabilizing a hooked knee to a beast's ribcage; a jabbed heel crunching into a hog's bent leg joint; an ear bitten here, a head butted there, a neck wrapped in a crushing choke hold. She smelled their eggy breath in her nostrils, tasted their soil-and-shit scent on her tongue. Parker wasn't merely ready for this final confrontation; she was excited for it. Amped. Ecstatic. Ravenous.

But even as her blood thrummed with slavering anticipation, her heart winced at her motivation. Not to bury herself in the mindlessness of the kill, or to punish herself with more injuries and exhaustion. She was going to save a town from a common enemy, to rescue people she barely knew, and, until what Sylvie told her last night, she'd assumed pretty much hated her. Were these people really worth risking her life for? Going into the lion's den like this, ill-prepared and practically blind? She could have convinced Sylvie to wait for the rangers' helicopter. That woman wasn't the only one who knew how to use her wiles to get what she wanted. Parker could have resisted, insisted; they could still be curled up in bed right now, spooning and kissing and caressing and loving. But Parker made this choice, to be a hero, and so here she was, trudging down a dark tunnel, trying not to trip on decades-old cart tracks, taking her hero's walk directly into senseless danger.

Still, the villagers of Hekla Lake didn't have to take Parker in like they had. Jimmy didn't have to let her fight; as much as she was an entertaining spectacle, she was sort of bad for business, an unbeatable contender, embarrassing burly manly men backwards and forwards. Cob Kulla didn't have to rent a room to her, cut her a deal on the rent and let her make up the rest by helping out at the bar every now and again. Lucy Delgado didn't have to toss Davey a treat every time she brought the week's mail, or make such a cheery deal out of the junk mail and catalogs that were the only pieces Parker ever got. Patty didn't have to start rotating in pork shoulder on her weekend menu, just because Parker had offhandedly mentioned she preferred it to short ribs.

The villagers of Hekla Lake had done right by Parker, and she was too busy building and insulating her coffin to notice or appreciate them. Well, enough of that bullshit. She was going to release them from this hell, and re-introduce them to Hel, the Viking Goddess who would save their asses, and then get to know them, outside of beating them up in the ring.

No sooner had this conviction tremored down Parker's spine than the tracks on the tunnel floor gave way to rocks that gleamed a burnt black-red with heat. As she stepped gingerly along the path, she had to move quickly, lest the bottoms of her shoes melt. She must be walking over Hekla's namesake lake now, the stream of ignited lava rocks that were the reason for the mine's shutdown in the first place. She considered turning around, regrouping with Sylvie (maybe trading shoes), and trying her luck down the other pathway. But then the walls glowed ahead, and she ducked around a bend into a low tunnel she had to stoop through, its path illuminated by torches protruding from the walls in stone sconces.

By the time this path finally opened into a rounded alcove, Parker was practically crawling on her knees, keeping herself upright only out of a desire not to burn any more of herself than she had to. In the alcove, she straightened up and was hit with a gust of hot air, like the fiery breath of a dragon, pluming out of an archway to her right.

Garish blue-and-orange light emanated from beyond the archway, and metal sounds clanged out of it, reverberating inside the alcove. Parker tiptoed over to investigate, peering through the doorway.

She was looking into a kind of forge. It was a large cavern, but not tiered as Sylvie had said the hogs' mine was. The cave's ceiling rose high and disappeared into shadow. The walls were lined with torches, and someone had constructed shelves and apparatuses Parker didn't fully comprehend. Stalagmites spiked out of the ground at intervals, some used to prop up workstations, others to mark stops for the mining carts that were pushed along the tracks from one tunnel to another on either side of the space. Dirt-caked humans pushed the carts, while plump, hairy, feral hogs guided them to the various workstations. There, more humans toiled, banging and clinking and clanging away at the ice-blue ore that was carted to them. They smelted the material in vats, then passed it along the assembly line, sweating profusely over their work as they shaped the softened ore into thin discs, and used precision chisels to etch markings into the fronts and backs of the discs.

Parker decided to clear this room first.

The torches cast plenty of deep shadows for Parker to disguise her entrance; she sidled like a crab through the archway and crouched behind a stalagmite. One of the villagers at the smelting vat peered through the steam and clocked her. She held a finger to her lips to silence him. He blinked a bead of sweat from his eyelash, and looked back down at his toils.

She observed the pattern of work for another sweltering minute, and then unsheathed the kitchen knife from her beltloop. As quietly as she was able, she crept out of her hiding space and stole up behind a feral hog with its back to her. Just as quietly, she slipped the blade into its hide, angled up under its ribcage to pierce its heart. She held its muzzle with her other hand and squeezed the hog as its body jerked in the throes of death. The villagers at the vat the hog was commanding gaped but kept silent. Parker dragged the hog's body behind her stalagmite and dropped it in the shadows, pulling the knife out only after they were hidden.

A second feral hog accompanying one of the villagers pushing a cart of ice-blue coins into the tunnel on the opposite wall swiveled its meaty head around as it walked. Its ears perked up and it hitched to a stop as it spied the guard-less villagers at their vat. It squawked something at them, but the sound was even, curious rather than alarmed.

Parker army crawled around the stalagmite, moving toward the vat. From its position, the feral hog couldn't see her, but another hog must have turned its attention her way because suddenly one of the villagers came around the vat and started shouting at a beast she couldn't see. He was shouting nonsense words, and curses, and making a general spectacle of himself. His distraction worked; both the hog Parker was crawling toward, and the guard she couldn't see, hoofed it to him and started kicking his legs out. With their attention on him, Parker was able to tuck herself in between the vat and the villagers' workstation.

"Psst," she whispered to the remaining villager. He was vaguely familiar, but with the amount of dirt caked on his face under a sheen of sweat, even if she did know him, he would be unrecognizable. "Get low and make for that exit over there. After you emerge, follow the tunnel on the left. Sylvie will get you out. Go now!"

The villager didn't need to be told twice. He dropped to his hands and knees and crawled back along the path Parker had taken to get herself here. He disappeared into the shadows by the stalagmite. Parker could only hope he reached the archway.

Finished with their beating, one of the hogs returned to its work of commanding a team of etchers at the chisel station, and the other escorted the beaten villager back to the vat. Its eyes registered shock when it noted the other villager was missing, but Parker didn't give it the opportunity to squeal. She lurched up and stabbed her knife through its chin, pinning its tongue to the roof of its mouth, and thrusting the blade up into its brain cavity. She swiftly removed the blade, its blood splattering her arm, and wrestled the twitching body to the ground. She tucked it away into her hiding spot between vat and workstation, whispered her escape instructions to the injured villager, and turned toward her next victim as the man hobbled into the shadows.

At the first etching station, Parker managed to sneak up behind the guard hog and slit its throat with no trouble at all. There were four villagers here, only one she recognized as the owner and operator of the grocery shop, and they quietly dropped their chisels, raced into the shadows, and followed her directions out of the forge. Parker wiped the bloody knife against her sleeve, and pressed on.

She had to cross the cart tracks to reach the next vat station, where two hogs grunted low to each other, seemingly holding their own conversation while two villagers shoveled ore into and out of the molten embers. This is where things went tits up.

As Parker took a diving roll across the tracks, a hog emerged from the delivery tunnel. Spotting her, it stopped short, and the cart being pushed by the villager behind it crashed into its rear end. The hog splayed out onto tracks, the cart tipped over, noisily spilling its cache of ore, and the villager yelped. Before the hog could scramble to its feet, Parker launched herself at it, getting it into a choke hold and jamming her knife into its ear. The blade punctured its brain, it kicked its final death-throe kick, and she pulled her knife back out. Only the blade snapped on its skull or some cartilage or something, and it came out truncated, useless.

Warning squeals erupted through the forge. So much for stealth.

Parker leapt to her feet. "Villagers, run that way! Take a left after the archway, and get the hell out of here!"

As she spoke, she ran. She bypassed the two guard hogs at the vat in favor of the one escorting a cart of discs through the opposite tunnel. It had smartly deduced that fighting her here would be wasteful, the better tact being to escape the room itself and alert its hogmates to her intrusion. As it pivoted toward the tunnel, she dove at its hindlegs, catching one ankle in her fist, the other hoof kicking her across the jaw. She ignored the pain, tugged the hog hard, and landed a left-handed gut punch. The nails between her knuckles tore into its entrails; she pulled back and struck three more times in rapid succession. The nails broke off as its stomach broke open, and she left it to die in agony as she turned back to the others.

The two hogs at the vat encroached on her, assessing and plotting. Beyond them, two more hogs were trying to round up the fleeing villagers, and a fifth and final hog raced toward the delivery tunnel. Parker zeroed in, took the hammer from her belt, and flung it like a hatchet at the running hog's back. The blunt end connected with its spine, hobbling it, but only briefly. It was enough time for Parker to dodge and weave around the two vat hogs. When she got to the escaping hog, it wheeled on her, goring her thigh with one of its tusks and snapping its teeth around her knee. She cried out but kept her wits – and her balance. She punched her nail-knuckles into its face, taking out both eyes and thoroughly fucking the beast up before the nails broke off inside its cheeks. She stomped on its head for good measure, and turned around just in time to catch two back-hooves to the pelvis.

As she crumpled over, she spit up a little, mostly water and little bit of apple. The hog had the gall to be disgusted, making a rude gesture with its frothing tongue, before following up its punt attack with a headbutt to her dropped shoulder. She pushed into it, deflecting the charge and forcing it back closer to one of the vats. Meanwhile, the second guard hog had looped around, and charged at her open flank. She took a tusk to the bicep, and countered with a punch to its face to dislodge its teeth.

"Here, piggy piggy!" A villager shouted. The hog that Parker had pushed back twisted bodily at the call. The villager let out a mighty battle cry and reached out with her bare hands to upturn the vat of molten embers. By the time the hog realized what was happening, it was too late: the embers splashed onto its snout and chest, and its hooves slipped on the sweating ground as it tried to back up. It became stuck under the flow of the stuff, its dying wails consumed by the liquid fire.

Parker mouthed a thank you, the villager winked, and then spun back toward the exit. She saw that the other villagers had taken down the guard hog that had been trying to wrangle them back to their workstations. It lay on its side near the archway, half engulfed in shadow, its head staved in and its tongue lolling in a pool of its own blood.

That left one hog for Parker to deal with, and it knew it. As Parker got to her feet, the remaining hog, shaking off the blow to its noggin, stepped back a pace. Its eyes roved the forge, clocking the exits, weighing its options. Parker thought of Ol'Onesie, the mistake she'd made in empathizing with its pain, and tsked at the hog.

"Not your day, my friend," she told it. It seemed to understand, and peeled off, making a desperate lunge toward the delivery tunnel. She body-slammed it, launching it into the wall. It bounced with a crunch and rolled back onto its feet. Snarling, it charged at her. She sidestepped its advance and kneed it in the neck. It whirled, kicking out with its hind hooves. Parker knocked the hooves away with the heel of her hand, and brought her boot down on the hog's head. It stumbled, legs scrambling for purchase. Parker threw a one-two combo at its face, then boxed its ears and twisted it into a triangle chokehold. On the ground, with its neck between her knees, she jerked, snapping its vertebrae. One more twitch, and the hog stilled.

Parker sat on the ground, catching her breath. She was bleeding pretty badly from the gouge in her thigh, but didn't have time to properly bandage up the wound. Instead, she took the nylon rope from her belt and tied it above the puncture. It would buy her some time, even if it did also make her leg numb.

At any moment another cart full of ice-blue nuggets would come through the delivery tunnel, pushed by a beleaguered villager escorted by a feral hog. Or else Parker's interlude had clogged up the labor flow; the carts that were meant to go into the far tunnel with their etched discs didn't make it, and so couldn't be unloaded in whatever cave lay beyond, and thusly sent back to the mine to be refilled with raw material. Either way, a hog was going to come into this cave soon, from one or other of the tunnels. Parker needed to get moving, but she couldn't decide which tunnel to take. It stood to reason that the mine in which Sylvie'd been imprisoned was down the delivery tunnel, but the other tunnel could lead to another cave like this one, where more villagers toiled, doing whatever-the-hell with the refined discs.

She decided to check that cave. If it was a room like this one, she could clear it out quickly, perhaps with some help from however many villagers worked there. If more hogs came up the delivery tunnel while she was away, maybe they'd be too confused to sound the alarm right away. They might assume the villagers had revolted and follow their trail back out the exit, where they'd meet up with Sylvie, who was angry enough that Parker was certain she could handle at least two, maybe even three hogs on her own, and more if the villagers who'd escaped were still there to help out.

Ducking behind a cart loaded with discs, she pushed it along the track, staying low. The track curved and dipped sharply down. She had to grip the cart tightly and brace her legs to keep from losing it. Her injured leg screamed but she held steady. The rattle of the cart's ungreased wheels reverberated through the tunnel, announcing her arrival as light grew ahead. As the track levelled out, she shoved the cart and released it, so that it broke into the room ahead of her. When it was not immediately beset by hogs, she tiptoed to the mouth of the tunnel and peered around its lip.

Here, the ceiling reached up and up and up, ascending like a stone cathedral. The cart track ran like a bridge over a wide, bubbling cauldron of black water. Streams trickled down the cavern walls from heights un-seeable. The light in the room came not from torches, but from the ore that pebbled the walls, glinting ice blue, refracting off the water and filling the room with an icicle haze. It smelled swampy, like salty sewage, and it was hotter in here than in the forge. Parker resisted the urge to shed layers, knowing – or hoping – she'd soon be back out in the cold, fresh air of the village.

No hogs or villagers occupied the space. A few feet out across the bridge, blocks laid across the track would stop the cart automatically. Beside this, there was a lever. Parker's cart had stopped only a little ways into the cavern. She got up behind it and pushed the cart out to this marker, then stopped and looked around.

There was no one here to rescue and no hogs here to hit. She should retrace her steps up the sloping cart track, race back through the forge, and continue on down the delivery tunnel, to the mine, where everyone waited to be saved or killed. But this space held her rapt, the gleaming walls, chocked full of the ore the hogs were forcing humans to collect in their mine, and the steaming lake, so black and ponderously boiling. Was this Hekla's Lake? An actual lake, rather than a metaphor? Why didn't the hogs collect ore from this cavern, when it so clearly teemed with the stuff? Why did they refine their collected ore so particularly in the forge, and then cart it in here, to this spot?

Before she could second-guess herself, Parker pulled the lever. It creaked and cranked into place. The blocks retracted. The wheels of the cart rolled forward and locked with a click. After a few uneventful seconds, Parker worked out that she needed to push the lever back, so she did, and the track broke apart with a clang. Parker stepped back as the track split, the portion the cart was on tilting to the side. It groaned and spun slowly, until the cart was upended enough for the discs to spill out. They plopped into the bubbling water, which burped at receiving them. Steam hissed up, and the odor expanded, and the gurgling glugged and glurped. Then the track twisted back, righting the cart and snapping itself back into place. Another click, and the cart was released. The blocks protruded back up to stop the next cart.

Parker's eyes slid around the cavern, waiting for something to happen. After a time, she shrugged. "Huh," she said. She wasn't sure what any of this meant, but at least now she had something to tell Sylvie, to help them piece together a new theory.

On her way back down the track, a tremor ripped through the cavern. Parker braced her feet, waited it out. But the tremor's intensity only increased, rocking her from side to side on the track. Bits of ore broke off from the cavern walls, tumbling into the burbling lake. Parker dropped to her knees and began crawling back toward the tunnel. Water splashed up onto the track, knocking into her like waves, and she slipped, her chin banging painfully against a rail. The water burned through her coat like acid and scarred her flesh. She scrambled, moving faster, slipping along as more and more ore nuggets quaked loose, their strange light extinguished as each plopped into the water.

When she reached the mouth of the tunnel, Parker found her feet. She looked back out across the cavern, watched as the water ate the track, pulling the cart into its depths. It bubbled and bubbled, and the cavern groaned and trembled, and Parker thought she saw something rising through the water. Something darker than the water itself, an eclipse of shadow swelling toward the surface. Something big.

Parker turned and ran up the track.

In the forge, vats and workstations had overturned, carts and their raw materials and refined ore scattered about, the hog carcasses dancing on the ground as the cave spasmed. Rocks broke loose from the cave walls, and stalactites cracked off from the ceiling. She narrowly dodged one that fell in her path, kept running. Somehow, she'd caused a cave-in. Curiosity killed the cat. Parker hated cats.

Down the delivery tunnel, she raced. This tunnel was also illuminated by ensconced torches inlaid into the wall, but some had fallen to the ground, knocked loose by the tremors, or else their flames had been extinguished by dirt that cascaded down the walls with each quake. The track dipped and curved, and Parker tripped over her own feet a few times, throwing herself into a graceful gymnast's tumble as if she'd meant to do it. Finally, she did a forward handspring into the light at the end of the tunnel and found herself plop in the middle of the feral hogs' mine.

Here, chaos reigned.

The cavern was vast, far more enormous than she imagined from Sylvie's description of it. The stalagmites were twice as large and four times as girthy as she was, and they were splitting open, coming apart as the tremors tore through the mine. The myriad staircases lining the cavern walls and the platforms that made up the mine's tiers were coming apart as well, the stone and clay crumbling under the pressure of the quakes, or else exploding under the weight of fallen stalactites.

Villagers ran helter-skelter through the space, searching for an exit, dodging falling debris, and evading the feral hogs squealing and chasing them, trying to round them back up. Many villagers were fighting the hogs now, using their picking tools as weapons. There was dirt and blood and sweat and screaming, and everywhere the foul smells of shit and fear.

Parker put her fingers in the corners of her mouth and loosed a sharp whistle.

All eyes, human and hog alike, turned to her. She waved her arms at the tunnel behind her. "This way!" she shouted. It was all she had time to say before a hog lurched into her periphery. She brought her leg up to block as it threw itself into her flank. She grabbed onto it, and they rolled together down the sloping track, coming to rest at the base of a stalagmite that was still mostly intact.

Parker saw human feet race by her as she tussled with the hog. It got in a few good nips and kicks before she quelled it by elbowing it so hard in the snout that its nose bone dislodged and pierced its brain. She left the body and limped into the fray.

"Good on ya, Parker!" shouted Patty, who swatted a feral hog in the butt with the flat end of her shovel as it attempted to skirt by her on a beeline for Parker. Annoyed, it turned its attention back to her, and she froze.

"Bend and stab!" Parker yelled at her. "Bend and stab, Patty!"

Patty dropped to one knee just in time. She brought the shovel point-out like a javelin, and the hog rammed straight into it, the spade breaking off in its neck. Its momentum knocked Patty to the ground, and its body slumped over her. Parker got to them just as Patty pushed the beast off of her, awash in its blood, laughing her head off.

"Holy fuck," she announced. "But that was satisfying!"

Parker fetched a pickax off the ground and thrust it into Patty's eager hands. "Get them out of here. The place is coming down."

Patty saluted, then raced off, swinging madly at a cluster of hogs that circled a copse of terrified villagers. Parker didn't even have time to flinch when one of the hogs dodged Patty's swing and gored her under the armpit. A sob or a scream or a hard lump of vomit caught in Parker's throat.

There was so much blood, and soon, there would be no more Patty.

Parker stumbled back. Everywhere she looked, there were hogs. They seemed to pour out of the shadows and materialize in the dust kicked up from debris. Villagers fought them off the best they could as they made their collective way to the exit tunnel. Giving up on wrangling the people back into submission, the hogs were goring to kill, trampling and ramming and mauling with violent abandon. Not everyone was going to make it out of this mine unscathed, or even at all. Parker's only goal at this point, then, was to draw the attention of the feral hogs to herself. It was too late for her to save Patty, but she had to try to buy the other villagers more time and spare as many of them as she could.

To that end, she started picking up fallen stones and hurling them at packs of hogs. She shouted and leapt behind carts and atop breaking stalagmites, chucking stones and tools at the masses, taunting the hogs with hand gestures and lewd comments as she vaulted up an intact staircase. On a rock ledge, she braced her back against the quaking cave wall and aimed her ammunition at the hogs who finally turned and started back toward her position. Some were intercepted by armed villagers, others fell victim to crushing debris, but still more made it to the staircase, and mounted the steps in pursuit of Parker.

She locked her knees and faced her adversaries, a teeming wall of feral hogs, spittle flying from their maws, ears red with rage. Along the way, she'd picked up a garden scythe. Now, she crossed the staff in front of her and squared off with the hoard like a gladiator facing her opponent atop Mount Olympus. The hogs pressed toward her as a pack, but the ledge was too narrow; one hog squeezed ahead, and Parker sliced her scythe at its neck. She clipped its shoulder, but it was enough of a hit to knock the beast off balance. With a wild squeal, it tumbled off the ledge and fell to the lower level of the mine, where it lay in an unmoving heap.

The press of hogs continued forward, forcing Parker to take careful, sliding steps in retreat. She swiped at the hogs that got their noses too close to her, but they stayed back far enough not to lose their balance and follow their brethren to a similarly plummeting fate. The ledge cut right and widened out, opening up into an irregularly shaped landing that was crisscrossed with cart tracks. The tunnel openings were now blocked by boulders, and a curving wall was dotted with smaller openings, boulders blocking their entrances but in a more purposeful way. Parker figured these were some of the cells the villagers had been kept it, the boulders moved in front of them to act as doors, trapping the villagers inside. The boulders in front of the track tunnels, however, were more likely the result of the former cave-in that shut down the original mine.

At the far end of the oval, the ledge tapered back in, and curled inward to meet up with another staircase. These steps were shattered by falling rocks, and piles of rock and clay built up here where it still fell from fissures in the cave ceiling.

Parker positioned herself in the center of the oval and faced the oncoming throng. Her thigh throbbed, and her fingers flexed around the staff of the scythe. She made eye contact with the leader of the hoard, and blew it a kiss. It snorted, clapped heads with its neighbors, and they charged as one.

Before she was completely overrun, Parker put in a good show. She scythed through the initial wave of feral hogs like butter statues tossed haplessly in her lap, offering themselves up for the carving. She took one hog's head clean off, and hooted in triumph, extremely disappointed that no one saw that. Hooves came off at the ankle, stomach slit open to release steaming intestines, ears and tails and tusks lopped off, and still the hogs surged forward. Using carcasses as shields or launching pads as needed, Parker did a pirouette around the landing, a lethal ballerina, more deadly than graceful. Her dance instructor would be proud (or horrified, whichever).

Distantly, Parker was aware the ceiling was collapsing, the walls cracked apart. Torches quaked out of their sconces, the flames finding the wooden carts to eat. Tongues of fire licked at the ice blue ore and shot up happy sparks as they consumed the gems. An unsettling rumble growled through the hollow space, filling the cavern with its roar. Most of the humans had escaped, or were escaping, but pockets of folks were trapped by feral hogs, desperate to kill that which they could no longer command. Bodies, both beast and man, littered the cavern floor. Everyone was in a bad way, not least of all Parker herself.

Swinging the scythe became more trouble than it was worth. The blade's edge dulled, barely gouging through the thick hides of the hogs now. Parker switched it up, leading with her left arm and clocking hogs with the wooden end of the scythe staff. She concussed a few, knocked several more off the landing, and stabbed one in the eye, whereupon she lost the scythe altogether as the hog stumbled back to the rim of the ledge, taking the weapon with it. More hogs pushed in, obscuring Parker's view of the stabbed hog's final plunge.

Once again surrounded, Parker no longer had the advantage of a blade. She had only her fists and her wits. But as she rolled her neck slowly from shoulder to shoulder, flexing her casual largess to intimidate the hogs, she realized Shame and Loathing had no place in this cave. Parker didn't feel either of those emotions here in this moment, and hadn't felt them since saving Sylvie out in the national park. What she actually felt was good, imbued with purpose, her muscles singing with renewed passion. She shook out her hands, cracked her knuckles. As she raised her fists before her, staring over her taped-up fingers at the many pairs of onyx eyes that glared back at her, she re-christened her most precious assets: Triumph and Glory.

The next few minutes were a tornado of punches, kicks, elbows, teeth, and tusks. Parker lost track of all else outside of her own body; she followed the rhythm of her heart as it pumped adrenalized blood through her arms and legs. She ignored the pain of blows landed against her in favor of focusing on the muscles contracting and releasing in her limbs as she fought. The crush of hog bodies was the only thing that kept Parker upright in the center of the melee; every time she keeled, another head butted her back up, or a backside slammed her spine straight. She reached a point of exhaustion where she could no longer continue on the offensive; all of her strength and cunning went into blocking blows and dodging bites, keeping herself from being pinned to a point of no return. But it was so much – too much.

At least most of the villagers got out, she thought. Sylvie will get them to safety, and the mine will collapse in on itself, taking all of these infernal hogs with it. Hadn't Parker come to Hekla Lake to bury herself, after all?

Just as she had given up, her arms falling limply to her sides as she let her knees sink to the ground, scraping against the tusks that pressed in to hold her up, a rock exploded against the backside of one of the hogs. More rocks exploded in rapid succession until finally the pressure of all those heaving hog bodies lightened up as, one by one and then all together, they turned toward the incoming projectiles.

At the ledge they'd come from stood Jimmy Hogan, of Jimmy's Gym, naked as the day he was born, gleaming with sweat and dirt, huffing out breath like he was in desperate need of a ventilator. Beside him stood Barbara Mountain Seeker, hucking rocks at the hogs, mostly connecting, whooping with wild-eyed delight when she did.

"Oy, you greasy fucks!" Jimmy egged the hogs closer to him. Parker, on her knees now and useless to the pair, tried to shout for them to run. The hogs were closing in, and as heroic as their efforts were, in hand-to-hand combat against the feral beasts, Jimmy and Mountain Seeker didn't stand a chance.

But Parker's shouts were wasted. The two had a plan. When the hogs got just close enough,

Mountain Seeker threw her head back and boomed out. "Now!"

From the third-tier pathway above them, a boulder as large as a school bus came rolling down. Most of the hogs didn't even have time to turn and gape before it crushed them, like so many shit-covered pins in a really disgusting bowling alley. The force of the boulder cracked through the landing, continuing on down to the mine floor, taking the splattered hog bodies with it. A large chasm now separated Parker from the other two, who were both looking across it at her, grinning from ear to ear.

She grinned back. Above her she heard cheering coming from the villagers who had pushed the boulder over the edge. Parker blinked blood from her eyes, and waved her thanks at Jimmy and Mountain Seeker, which was all she had the strength to do.

"Yo!" Jimmy shouted over. "How do you punch these things all the time, Eriksen?" He lifted up his arms, his hands hanging defeatedly. "I think I broke both my wrists!"

Mountain Seeker cuffed him on the shoulder, and turned him around to go back the way they'd come. "Can you climb down, Parker?" she called. "I don't think this place is going to last much longer!"

Parker nodded, found her voice. "I got this," she lied.

When they were out of sight, Parker lay down atop the nearest feral hog carcass to join it in death.

Chapter Eight

It is said that right before you die, time slows down, and you relive the greatest moments of your past, or the worst, the most memorable, at any rate, or maybe it's random. It's generally a good feeling, swimming through the past before you drown, getting the chance to say goodbye to your life before you go under forever. This, however, was not Parker's experience.

Parker's dying breath didn't exhale her back through flashes of the past, but propelled her into the future, or into a possible future, like a generous ghost who'd made a pitstop on its way to meet up with Mr. Scrooge.

The smells of this not-memory hit Parker first, filling her mouth with the stinging taste of saliva, pushing out the salted flavor of her own blood.

Fresh baked chocolate chip cookies, spiced apple cider, crisp fallen leaves. Next came a vision in red: Sylvie Cahwee, walking toward her, wearing a knee-length red velvet dress, cut low to highlight an immaculate neckline, sleeves to her wrists, adorned with silver bangles. In her holiday oven-mitted hands, she held out a tray of cookies to Parker, blew hot air between her lips, trying to scoot the pom of her Santa hat that had fallen in front of her face.

"Can you taste these, babe?" Sylvie asked, proffering the tray. "I think I used too much flour."

The cookie was soothingly warm in Parker's hand – a hand that was unbroken, unscarred, skin as smooth as a baby's bottom, no swollen knuckles, no disjointed wrist. Her nails were even painted like candy canes. The cookie was chewy, and yes it had too much flour, but Parker ate it greedily, and scooped up a second before Sylvie whisked the tray away, laughing.

"I guess I'll take that as a five-star rating!" She laid the tray on the stovetop, took off the oven mitts, and stirred a pot with a wooden spoon. The spiced scent of apples wafted through the kitchen.

It was an enormous chef's kitchen, all white and stainless steel.

"Is this our house?" Parker asked. Her voice sounded strange to her; she'd lost some of the gravelly undertones, shed the jagged notes like a boxer trying to make weight.

At the stove, Sylvie tittered. "You with your dad jokes. I get it, it's never been this clean, yeah yeah. Are you going to get dressed? Your parents will be here any minute."

If she wasn't already dying, that information would have laid Parker flat. She thought she'd been carried into a pleasant dream of her could-have-been future, but now she feared she'd been tricked into a nightmare.

As is the nature of dreams, she suddenly found herself in an expansive living room, decorated with plush furniture and monochrome features. A silver Christmas tree sparkled in one corner, catching the light from the bay window on its wrap of rose gold garland. Cheerful piano music filled the space, emanating from the dining room just beyond a columned archway. There at the baby grand piano sat her father, pounding away at the keys, as Parker's mother stood beside him, hands delicately resting upon his shoulder, chin up and belting out "O Holy Night."

Parker's skin jumped when someone touched her. It was Sylvie, coming up behind her to hug her from behind. She stood on her tiptoes to tuck her chin into the crook of Parker's neck, breathed deeply of her scent, which Parker only just then noticed was a perfume that reminded her of roasted chestnuts and candied cranberries.

"Isn't this lovely?" Sylvie kissed Parker's shoulder. Parker hugged Sylvie's arms to her and sighed into the embrace. This was lovely, yes. Being with Sylvie, having her close and happy and bursting with love. But this setting was all off, the addition of her parents, done up in austere Christmas garb, churning through classic carols as if trying to win a bet. In this house, which didn't fit her, which felt like Trondheim, like the posh apartment in Boston, like everything she'd grown to despise. If this was the future Parker was avoiding by dying now, in this weird feral hog mine, then maybe it was for the best.

In a blink, the scene changed, and Parker's rattling inhale cast her into another possibility. Here, she saw herself as if she were watching a film. The colors were muted, sepia-toned, all browns and beiges and yellowed whites. Film Parker was chopping wood by the side of a barn; the air was moist but not cold, the ground a bit sodden with recently-fallen rain. Film Parker made clean, even chops through the logs, stacking the bisected bits neatly in the covered log bin. She paused in her work, looked up at the overcast sky, and leaned against her axe, wiping sweat from her forehead with the back of her hand.

A familiar bark preceded Davey into the shot. He bounded in on his three little legs, butt wagging his dismembered tail. He trotted circles around Film Parker as she attempted to pet him or to pick him up, happily yipping and sniffing the chopping stump. He peed on the axe, and then ran out of the shot. Film Parker mock-yelled at Davey in admonishment, shook her head gleefully, and returned to her work.

Parker, watching this, felt her chest tighten, anticipating Sylvie's entrance into the scene. But she didn't come. Film Parker finished chopping the wood, cleaned up the splinters, put the axe away, and exited stage right. Parker was left with only the soft sounds of nature: chirping birds, whistling wind through unseen trees, creaking old barn settling in for winter. She smelled hay and grass and a nearby woodfire. Well, this was pleasant enough, even without Sylvie. She had Davey, after all, and seemed to be doing okay on this farm, assuming it belonged to her. Even if she was working for someone else, she was staying active, doing the physical labor that kept her sane, helped her feel alive. But of course, she wasn't alive, or nearly wasn't, and so it didn't really matter if this scene would ever play out in real life. It wouldn't. Just as well. Parker hated winter.

Another shift, static shooting across Parker's vision, air leaving her lungs once more, though it was getting harder to push it out, painful to suck it back in. She was back inside her body, and her body was pressed against the ropes of a fighting ring, hands clapping against each other, chalk dust puffing to the floor. Inside the ring, a young woman in training gear bobbed about on her toes, eyes boring into her opponent, another young woman in identical gear.

"Watch her feet, watch her feet!" Parker called. She was excited, and anxious. Around her, the sounds of a gym popped like firecrackers: the rapid thwack of someone working the speedbag, the clang of improperly dropped weights, the grunts and heaves of folks pushing themselves through a circuit. Slowly, the smells layered on, talc and sweat, ammonia and rubber, deodorant and feet.

In the ring, the women threw punches, blocked knees, landed kicks and elbows. They danced together and sprung apart. Parker cheered and shouted tips and encouragements, admonishments when needed. At the end of the sparring match, she was sweating almost as much as the fighters were. Both approached her, taking their mouthguards out to beam at her.

"How was that, coach?" One asked.

Parker felt her face loosen as a smile spread across it. "Much improved, Anderson. But you gotta watch your back after your fly kick. You're leaving yourself wide open. And Tykowski, I'm loving that one-two combo, but your feet need work. Overall, I'm happy. Don't I look happy? Hit the showers, I'll see you both in the morning for warm-ups."

As the girls left the ring, playfully swatting at each other and giving each other companionable shit, Parker noted the words emblazoned in fine black calligraphy across the backs of their sports tanks: Parker's MMA Gym.

Pride inflated Parker's chest, even as her lungs refused to take in any more air. The vision faded – all of her vision faded – and in the darkness, Parker felt her body slacken. Something like regret clogged her throat. She couldn't swallow, couldn't breathe. Her own gym. Her own girls taking on the patriarchy one MMA match at a time. Showing the world she had more to give it, and more to take, too. Triumph and glory. Pride and power. Blood and sweat and tears. In the future that wasn't to be, she wasn't wasting these things on feral hogs, on backwater fights that didn't mean anything. She was paying it forward, helping girls meet their potential, doing it on her own, without her father's money or influence, without Sylvie's Christmas cookies, or Davey's yapping. That was something to regret, that she would never meet this goal, that she would never even get the chance to make this goal in the first place.

It felt like a good time for a deep sigh, but of course that was beyond Parker now. Except it seemed Scrooge's wandering ghost had one more gift to give her. Air flooded her lungs, too much air, making her gasp – and suddenly she was coughing, breathing enough to cough, rolled over and spitting up onto the bloody hide of a feral hog.

"Goddammit, Parker, you're as stubborn as you ever were."

Through gummy lids, Parker's blurred vision kaleidoscoped until the dark figure in front of her took on human features, became a person, a familiar one at that. Victoria Marshall. Coach Vic. Naked and beat up, she held Parker by the neck and shoulder, and smiled down at her.

"Am I hallucinating?" Parker croaked out.

Spittle flecked Vic's bottom lip as she guffawed. "If I'm the last thing you hallucinate before you die, I feel sorry as hell for you, kid."

With Vic's help, Parker sat up. The cavern filled with the loud sound of rocks coming apart from the walls and ceiling, crashing into other debris on its way to crush any hog or human too slow to escape its descent. Screams of agony and for help, squeals for much the same. Parker thought for a moment her eyes were wobbly, but it was the cavern itself, jostling about like a soda can in a toddler's vigorous grip. The space smelled of sulfur and shit, desperation and rot. Shakily, Parker got to her feet, helped along by Vic's nimble fingers under her elbows and a steadying hand at the small of her back.

"You good, Parker?" Vic stooped, trying to get a good bead on Parker's eyes, which roved about in confusion and not a little relief.

The last time she'd seen Coach Vic, she was standing in the front row of a Las Vegas arena, pumping her fists in the air and roaring along with the crowd as a referee paraded Parker around the ring in which she'd just pummeled a man twice her size to win the championship belt she now hoisted over her head like a fresh kill. It was that shining, bright face, full of pride and feeling, that Parker, after learning her entire career had been a farce, never wanted to see again. To see that look of teary-eyed admiration morph into pained disappointment, or worse, to hear Vic verbally express the same, tsking and casting her eyes down, denouncing her prized pupil, disowning her. Parker couldn't bear it, so she turned her own shame into anger, into blame, convinced herself Vic should have warned Parker more fervently, forbade her from going off and getting her ego all inflated, of joining up with a scoundrel like

Guillermo Reyes, of trusting her greasy-fingered father to stay well away from her business.

And now here she was, Coach Vic, as naked as all the other villagers, cut up and swollen, a black eye swallowing half her face, and limping on an ankle double the size of her other one. Picking Parker up out of the rubble of hog carcasses and collapsing rock, asking her if she can move, insisting on it, leading her over to the cavern wall. Rescuing her.

"Vic," Parker said, but couldn't think of how to follow that up. "Vic, what...? How...?"

"Less talking, more fleeing," Vic coached, and entwined her fingers for Parker to step onto her palms. She boosted her up and directed her on how to climb up the wall, which was broken up enough to provide decent hand and footholds. Parker scrambled, her body gone gooey, but whenever she faltered, Vic was right behind her to redirect. Parker may not have been dead, but she felt enough like a corpse to pass for one. Having a ghost from her past help her bare-knuckle up a cavern wall to escape a crumbling mine full of feral hogs commanding humans to collect a strange ore that they then forged into coins, etched with some kind of ancient runes, and then dumped into a volcanic underground lake for God knows what reason, wasn't exactly doing much to convince Parker she wasn't smack in the middle of the general delirium that preceded death.

When they reached the ledge of the third-tier, Vic led Parker around a curve, ducking and dodging debris. She held her body curled over Parker's, letting the smaller rocks ping onto her back and shoulders rather than hit Parker. Sooner than Parker expected, they reached their destination: an old cart tunnel, partially blocked by a cracked boulder. Whether it had been displaced by the intensifying quake, or pushed out of the way by brute human strength, Parker couldn't tell. There was enough of an opening for Parker to slip inside, nudged along by Vic who straightened up and followed after her.

The chaos was muted in the tunnel, the heat a little subdued. And if not for the torch Vic brought in with her from a sconce next to the tunnel entrance, it would be completely dark. Vic urged Parker forward through the narrow but high-ceilinged tunnel – shuffling along the cart track, which twisted and turned and angled gradually upwards.

Finally, Parker couldn't stand listening to the sound of her own ragged breath, Vic's strained wheeze, the slap of their uneven feet, the rumbling of the mountain in its own delirious death throes. "Vic, what are you doing here? How did you get here? How...I was dead."

"You writing an article?" Vic riffed. She lightened up, gave Parker's elbow a pleasant squeeze. "I saved your damn life, kid, you need to know more than that?"

"I always figured you were my Guardian Angel," Parker said.

Vic quirked a smile, which shadowed into a grimace by the light of the torch. "You got that right, kid. First, I save you from pooping pigeons, now industrious wild boar. What is it with you and animals?"

"Hey, I get along okay with dogs. I have one. Davey." Just thinking of him stirred a longing in her gut. Unless it was the talk of poop, churning her bowels awake. It'd been a long time since she voided, unless you counted all the vomiting.

"Cute. I hope you get the opportunity to introduce me."

Parker stopped walking, causing Vic to step on her heel. She looked at Vic, searching for answers without asking any questions. Then she said, "You were at Jimmy's."

Vic shrugged. "A regular sherlock, you."

"Bad luck. Should have come last month, or next." Or never, Parker thought. Never would have been best.

"Parker, I come to all your fights."

"What?"

The tunnel tremored, and more rock dust tumbled onto the track. The two resumed their hurried walk, the angle of the track growing steeper as it straightened.

"Heard a rumor about some Amazon woman gobbling men's balls in amateur fights out this way," Vic explained. "Part of me must have considered the possibility it was you. Hadn't heard or seen from you in months. Didn't even know if you were in the country. But a ball-eating Amazon? Worth the plane ticket to check it out; maybe I recruit some new meat. But when I got to the airport, there was this board with flyers and brochures advertising local entertainment, eateries, whatever. And there it was, a one-sheet buried under a stack of Dollywood coupons: The Viking Goddess Hel, sending men to the underworld."

Vic chuckled, and in that chuckle, Parker detected top notes of bemusement, infused with a healthy dose of awe.

"The one and only," Parker said, and drank down Vic's follow-up chuckle like the sweetest glass of water.

"Girl, I was floored," Vic went on. "I almost didn't go. I sat in my little motel room off the freeway, staring at that one-sheet, that photo of you with the Viking horns, the fur-lined boots with your little speedos." She shook her head, overcome with the memory. Parker gave her the space to recollect. "Maybe I wouldn't have gone to the match if the picture'd been different. If you'd looked, I don't know, happy in it. If it'd been you, not some character. I could have left you alone – I mean, you clearly wanted me to leave you alone – but that picture...It wasn't you, and curiosity got the better of me. I had to see who it was."

"I guess I didn't disappoint," said Parker. "I mean, you kept coming back."

"Five or six times, I'd reckon. And I've never been disappointed, not in you as a person or as a fighter. I was...I was mesmerized, and, to tell you the truth, a little frightened. In the ring, you fought well, of course you did, but there was no joy in it. Not like when you fought for me, or even when you..." She wouldn't say his name. "When you went into MMA. At Jimmy's, you fought like a zombie, to be honest, and it made me sad. Every time I came back to watch you, I thought maybe this time I'll say something. Maybe this time I'll come out of the shadows and confront you."

Parker needed time to process so she urged Vic on, "...but then?"

Vic sighed, the effort rattling something inside her chest. The torch flame whickered as her breath brushed by it. "But then I lost my nerve to approach you, yet again, and was looking forward to tucking my tail between my legs in a hot bath back at my motel, but the damn rental stalled out. A mechanic in the pub said she'd help me out after a pint, so I thought, what the hell, I'll have one too. A beer is the next best thing to a bath, right? Warms you up the same. Only, I never got to finish it. Everything went tits up, I blacked out, woke up in the mines with everyone else. Been trying to get a rebellion going, amass a revolt, you know, but then you showed up, you goddamn showed up, kid, and when you started laying into those hogs, I saw you, I saw you, Parker. My Parker. My champion."

So many emotions seeped into Parker's blood, so many questions rumbling up through her bones. No, not through her bones, through the tunnel floor.

A great, echoing CRACK resounded through the tunnel. As one, Parker and Vic looked down. A huge fissure ran between their legs down the path of the cart track, breaking the rails apart and hissing up steam. From the depths of the tunnel's darkness behind them, a gurgling roar croaked forth, followed a second later by a smog of moist, hot air that smelled of bile and uncooked bacon.

"Run!" Vic commanded, and Parker obeyed.

There was no talking on this sprint, this final lunge toward freedom. If this tunnel didn't open out into Hekla or the village's surrounding environs, Parker and Vic would be crushed to death in the mountain's collapse, or else eaten alive by whatever was chasing them (a pack of seriously pissed off feral hogs, by the sounds of it), or some combination of the two.

Vic led the charge and Parker followed her torchlight like a moth racing after a flame. She tried to distract herself from the pain thrumming through her body by going over the things Vic had revealed to her. She didn't know how to feel about any of it. It was only just last night, wrapped in Sylvie's bruising arms, ice packs on her wrists and ankles, softly breathing in the scent of her shampoo in Sylvie's hair, that Parker even started to come around to the idea that Hekla Lake maybe wouldn't be her final resting place. That maybe, by releasing the feral hogs' prisoners and dismantling their regime, she would metaphorically dismantle the coffin she'd constructed around herself, claw herself back up out of the dirt, and look forward to something – celebrating an intimate family Christmas with Sylvie; preparing for winter at the ol' homestead by chopping wood with Davey; coaching a sparring match at her own gym – instead of continuing to look over her shoulder at her receding past. Now, she was confronted with one of the largest elements of that past, a woman whose heart she had broken. And Vic wasn't even trying to forgive her, because, it seemed to her, there was nothing to forgive. All she seemed to want for Parker were the things Parker was finally starting to admit she might be able to have: a feeling of accomplishment again, of pride, of coming alive during a match and giving her all to her passion.

How was Parker supposed to respond to someone who wanted all of those things for her? Sylvie wanted those things for Parker, too, but she was different. She knew a truncated and diluted version of Parker's past, drunkenly confessed to her over pints one night, but she hadn't lived it with Parker. It wasn't part of her experience. If Vic wrote a memoir of her life as an amateur boxing coach, Parker would get an entire chapter, possibly even a whole sub-section, at the very, absolute least a lengthy annotated endnote. It was hard enough for Parker to accept and trust such kindness and encouragement from someone new in her life; to trust it from someone who had every reason to dismiss her? That might be asking too much.

Yet, here they were, running for their lives together, Vic once again leading her down a path out of darkness toward a bright future. Only this time it was literal; a dot of light winked at the pair from higher up the cart track tunnel, and cold air trickled in to nibble at their heated flesh. Vic gasped a cry of relief, and Parker whooped in celebratory anticipation. From behind them – much too close behind them – something large bellowed its throaty disappointment.

It was in this moment that Parker regretted her curiosity in the freshwater cavern. Whatever was chasing them, it was more than just a regular feral hog. Sylvie had been teasing, but maybe these things *were* hooyups; maybe the stories had bastardized their real purpose. Not stealing Grandma and Grandpa to eat them but to put them to work. Harvesting and etching and creating – what? A spell, some kind of ritualistic casting. By dumping those etched discs in the water, had Parker....Had she.... "Oh shit," Parker breathed. "I think I summoned something."

"What?" Vic wheezed.

As the light expanded wide enough to show them a glorious wintry scene beyond the tunnel opening, Vic tripped over a bit of broken track and fell on her face. The torch tumbled out of her hand

and extinguished against the rocks. Without its glow, it was difficult to see where the fissure was that had split the track and been zigzagging along faster than they could run. The light outside of the tunnel opening didn't penetrate the darkness within, and Vic was lost to thick shadows, shimmering like an oil slick as the mountain continued to quake.

"Vic!" Parker cried out. Her mind flashed visions of Vic spilling over the lip of the fissure, scraping her nails against the unforgiving rock as she was swallowed by the abyss.

"I'm here!" Vic called back. Parker found her with her feet, bent and flailed for her arms. "I think I broke something, my knee, or twisted it terribly. I don't know if I can stand up."

Parker ignored the groans and stabbing protests her own body made as she grasped Vic's arms and hoisted her up. "You can stand. I've got you. You can do this."

Vic leaned her considerable weight on Parker, who propped her up with an arm around her waist while Vic slung her own arm across Parker's shoulders. They limped forward, inching closer and closer to the outside.

That was when Parker made one of the biggest mistakes of her life: she looked behind her.

Fifty yards down the tunnel, illuminated by ice-blue runic etchings along its hide, was the face of a feral hog, impossibly large. It filled the space from side to side and top to bottom, was actually too big, its tusks acting as bulldozers as it pushed its way up the tunnel, carving out room for its gargantuan noggin. Its eyes burned ice blue, it's nose shiny with mucus, its mouth lolled open as it panted over a huge, slapping tongue. Parker didn't care to dwell too long on its teeth. She focused her head forward and tried to pick up the pace.

"What...what did you see?" Vic asked, trying to crane her own gaze around, but luckily too sore to get the angle right.

"Nothing, nothing." Parker gulped, tightened her grip on Vic, fisted the last dregs of her adrenaline, and ran, dragging Vic along the cart track.

They emerged into a field of snow, enclosed in a semicircle of frosted firs, spruces and pines, the national park stretching out before them. The snow was waist deep, and Parker had to let Vic go so they could both push their way through it. It didn't much matter how well either of their legs worked at this point; they crawled through the snow like little plows, not stopping until they reached the cover of the trees. Here, the snow flattened out to a manageable ankle height, and the two women pitched onto their stomachs, utterly spent.

Parker allowed herself three to four seconds to savor the taste of fresh air, the sting of the cold, the smell of bark and clear sky and pine needles. Then she scooped snow into her mouth to wet her gullet and soothe her chapped lips, and she turned around to wait for the beast to follow them out of the tunnel. She thought about reaching for Vic's hand, but didn't want her to panic at the uncharacteristic sentimentality.

Ancient wooden beams outlined the tunnel entrance. The snow on the mountain came down in great sheets, uprooting trees and crashing down around the base. It was a miracle Parker and Vic had avoided being crushed by all of that. As Parker watched, wide-eyed and ill-prepared, a tusk the size of a spruce tree stabbed through the tunnel, splitting the beams and bringing more of the mountain down. Then a second miracle happened:

cracks like thunder boomed out of the mountain, and suddenly it wasn't there anymore, disappeared in a cloud of snow and rock dust as the entire thing collapsed in on itself. The tusk, and the giant beast it was attached to, was buried.

Parker fell back onto the snow. She stared up at the cloudless sky and listened to Vic murmur delightedly beside her. Vic hadn't seen the tusk, hadn't even looked up when the mountain imploded. She was too busy sucking down handfuls of snow, rehydrating after so many days with only a piddling stream of hot piss-water to drink in the hogs' mine. She smacked her lips like it was the sweetest wine she'd ever tasted, mumbled praise and thank you's. Parker spread her arms out and then her legs, and then moved them slowly in and out, in and out, creating snow angels.

The stillness of the forest was overwhelming. It was as if existence had been sucked into a vacuum. The cacophonic symphony of the collapsing mine suddenly seemed a distant memory, or as if it had occurred in a separate reality, or to someone else, or in a slowly dissipating nightmare. Parker closed her eyes, regulated her breathing, and laid still as the soundless forest.

"Coach," she said after a time. Vic's murmuring ebbed, but she still slurped at the snow as she listened. "I have to tell you. I was ashamed. Like...a giant feral hog dogged my every step. It was always there, looming over me, breathing down my neck, reminding me of all the stupid shit I'd gotten myself into. All the lies I'd believed – from my father, from Ray, even from you. 'Cause that's what I thought, you see. That you all had lied to me, that everyone was putting me on, winding me up because Daddy paid them off, because it was entertaining, you know, to build someone up and then tear them down. And as I languished, kind of wishing the beating I'd taken in that alleyway had killed me, that shame just got bigger and bigger. Its huge, ugly shadow covered everything in front of me, and there was no way I could turn around and face the thing head-on. I had to try to outrun its shadow, at least that was my thinking. If I got far enough away, I could escape its reach. And then I could...I could, I don't know, lay down and die, but on my own terms, my own time. Because, Vic, I haven't been doing that, you know? Taking things on my own terms, in my own time. I haven't been, not even with you. And now I have to apologize because I'm not coming back to your gym, Vic, I'm not going anywhere, okay? Because I'm not your champion, I'm not your fighter, and even when I was, I wasn't, you know? Or I didn't want to be, not fully, and maybe that's why I didn't listen to your warnings about Ray. Maybe that's why I went with him, because I thought, well, I thought here was an opportunity to become more me, you know? Without you, and eventually, without him. But of course he wouldn't let me do that, and even if he had, my family wouldn't, my father – so, no, I'm not your champion. And thank you for saving me and everything, and for training me, and, and, I know it's shitty, I know I'm nothing, not really, but I have to try it, right? I have to try to be something, not for anyone else, but for me, inside the ring and outside of it, without my father's money, without Ray greasing palms, without any of it. So, I'm sorry, Vic, I'm so, so sorry."

At some point during her speech – which she hadn't intended to be a speech but all the words she'd held inside for over a year gushed free – Parker began to cry, heaving sobs racking out of her. She allowed Vic to wrap her shoulders in a comforting hug and kept on talking through the tears, feeling immense relief unlike anything she'd ever felt, purging her sins. If she stayed in Hekla Lake now, it would be her choice, not her penance. She breathed out with gusto, laughing and sobbing – she was free, she was free, she was free!

"Don't you dare apologize to me, kid," Vic said. She rubbed Parker's back, patted her knee. The cold didn't seem to bother her naked skin, in fact it seemed to buoy her: color returned to her cheeks, life to her eyes. Her breath stank horribly but Parker could forgive it. "First of all, everything that asshole Ray told you was utter bullshit. He didn't pay anyone off to fight you – every athlete in the business wanted to go up against you. Managers were throwing money at him, trying to get a match with you. Secondly, your father is a cunt, and if you're implying he paid me or Ray or anyone else to train or represent you, you're dead wrong. That snake tried to bribe me to cut you loose, to tell you that you were no good and had no future in the ring. He saw how incredible you were at your first bout, how much it filled you with passion and purpose, and he was terrified. The ring set you free, Parker. You found your true love. And even after everything, no one has been able to take that away, least of all you, hard as you try to cut yourself down." Vic held up Parker's fists, and kissed a knuckle on each hand. "You and these are a deadly combo, killing it no matter where you are, you got me?"

"Triumph and Glory," Parker said.

Vic grinned. "Triumph and motherfucking glory."

They smiled at each other as if nothing bad had ever separated them, mentor and mentee, eye to eye and fist to fist.

"Come on," she said, gripping Vic's elbow to help her up. "Let's get back to the village. You're gonna freeze out here."

Vic looked down at herself. "I completely forget I was butt ass naked."

This comment sent them, fits of giggling and belly laughs propelling them to their feet. As they turned to walk, arm in arm, deeper into the forest, in the direction Parker was fairly certain lay the fire tower and, beyond that, the valley that marked the edge of Hekla Lake, a great, rasping roar stopped them cold.

From the depths of the collapsed mine, a new mountain was forming. Parker and Vic watched, rapt, unable to unstick their quivering legs and get the hell out of there. Earth, snow, broken trees and rocky debris rose in three distinct clumps, up and up and up, until the cascading debris waterfalled enough to reveal what it was that was clawing itself up out of the pits of Hell: three coarse, brown hog heads with snarling, frothing snouts and gnashing teeth; three pairs of tusks swiping at each other, the gaping maws spitting and roaring as the heads shook off the remnants of the mine. Ice blue tattoos cut across the flesh, symbols shining through the hair like particularly bloodthirsty will-o'-the-wisps. Inside each set of eyes burned that unholy blue flame as one set of gargantuan hooves found purchase in the clearing and heaved the rest of the beast's bulk out of the hole.

When it was fully excavated, the three-headed monstrosity paused to collect itself. Each noggin the size of an industrial tractor, tusks like giant mulching blades gleaming yellow-white above the snow-covered ground, its bulbous body – easily the size of thirty to fifty feral hogs humped together – quaking off dirt, rocks, tree limbs and snow as it gazed around, assessing.

Parker felt Vic try to slink back, take cover behind a tree or disappear beneath the shadows of the forest canopy. But Parker held fast to the spot. There was no use running or trying to hide; the beast could smell them. Hot air billowed out of the thing's cavernous nostrils as it sniffed around. It locked on to the pair's location, all three heads swiveling to stare them down with six glittering blue eyes.

"Vic," Parker said out of the corner of her mouth. "If you can run on your own, do it. Keep going west until you hit the fire tower, then follow the snowmobile tracks to town. There's a park ranger there, Sylvie Cahwee, she's rounding up the surviving villagers. Get her attention and warn everyone, and then get out, however you can, just go until this accursed village is no more than a speck on a map in an airport brochure bin."

"Parker, you can't seriously take this thing on," Vic hissed.

Parker set her shoulders. "If not me, who else?" She didn't give Vic the luxury of thinking about it. The three-headed feral hog stomped its hooves, crouched into a lunge position. "I can at least buy you time. Now, go!"

Vic ran, as best she could, slushing ungracefully but forcefully through the snow, pitching handfuls of the fluff behind her as she fled.

Parker was alone with the beast.

As the feral hog trained its blazing gazes on her, ducking its heads to glare down its snouts at her, Parker stretched, breathing through the aches in her bones, the redoubled pulsing of her heart. She slotted her body into fighting position: shoulders relaxed, fists up, bouncing lightly on the balls of her feet. This was it. She was in the ring. Except Parker had nothing more to prove, not to herself or to anyone else, and she didn't feel grim about her odds of survival, or as if this were her only choice, to fight or to die. Parker could do anything, now that she was free.

Distantly, she heard the familiar patter of helicopter blades slicing the air, accompanied by a mighty yip. Her Davey, somewhere far behind her in the village, and her Goliath, directly in front of her, waiting for her to sling her shot.

Parker grinned.

The three-headed feral hog huffed, its snort exploding snow outward like a dynamite blast. It stamped its hooves, growled like thunder, and charged at her.

Parker held the beast's gaze, and stood her ground. Triumph.

And motherfucking glory...

The End.

Afterword

Fall 2020 was *rough.* I was terrified that I or my family would catch Covid-19, for which there wasn't yet a vaccine or adequate treatment. My mother was in hospice, slowly (but all too quickly) leaving us. Thoughts about my gender identity were no longer resting peacefully in the grave I had so generously dug for them. My seasonal depression was on the upswing. It was, simply, *a lot.*

And I couldn't fight any of it.

My normal escapes weren't working. My fear-swaddled brain had trouble focusing long enough on anything other than death to enjoy reading; I slept a lot, but my usually delightfully vivid dreams had become anxiety nightmares. Food remained a comfort, but even I got full eventually.

Thankfully, it was November. And November meant National Novel Writing Month.

If you don't know, National Novel Writing Month (or NaNoWriMo) is a writing program pioneered by Chris Baty, wherein you compete against your usual excuses to write a 50,000-word novel in 30 days. (You can learn more at nanowrimo.org)

I'd had success with NaNoWriMo 10 years prior, when I drafted EAT YOUR HEART OUT, my queer-women-vs-zombies novella, later published by BrazenHead (an imprint of Lethe Press). I wanted to try again. I *needed* to. I was aching for distraction, and this was it. There were no other options.

All I knew when I dove in on November 1st was that I was going to write about feral hogs. In 2019, I'd listened to unequivocally the most perfect episode of investigative journalism podcasting, "30-50 Feral Hogs" on Reply All (R.I.P.). As reported by Alex Goldman, the episode covered the deeper story behind this infamous pro-gun tweet:

William McNabb
@WillieMcNabb

Replying to @JasonIsbell

Legit question for rural Americans - How do I kill the 30-50 feral hogs that run into my yard within 3-5 mins while my small kids play?

11:01 AM · 8/4/19 · Twitter for iPhone

Thanks to Goldman's serious reporting on what began as an easily-panned tweet, I became utterly fascinated with feral hogs. I wanted to write about them, but not in any way that would require I do actual research.

I latched onto the idea of someone hunting feral hogs not with advanced weaponry but with their bare hands. Then I had some questions to answer: *how* is this character able to fight so well? *Why* is she fighting these hogs? *What* does she stand to lose if she stops (or if they win)?

Once I answered these questions for Parker Eriksen, everything else fell into place. The world around me was scary, sad and relentless, but the few hours I spent with Parker each day were fun, hilarious, and surprisingly *sincere*. This was a silly little horror story born from a silly little tweet, sure, but it evolved into something more along the way. Parker wasn't just punching feral hogs because the image made me giggle; Parker was punching feral hogs because she couldn't punch out her own anxieties and fears. (As the youths say: relatable content.)

My mom died on November 21st. I finally said out loud to my wife, "I think I'm trans." Audiobooks resurrected my ability to read. I finished the first draft of 30 TO 50 FERAL HOGS.

Many things since November 2020 have gotten worse, while some things have gotten better. I'm sure life is that way for you, too. It's my sincere hope that when you're feeling overwhelmed by it all, you can step into the ring with Parker Eriksen for a few hours, and come out swinging.

Dayna Ingram

Rural Ohio

March 2023

Acknowledgements

Thank you to Sarah and Rob, who made this book readable. Thank you Tom for your incredible cover art. Thank you Indie Horror Twitter, without this community I wouldn't have sought to publish...well, anything ever again. Thank you Catherine for your generosity and insights, to Steve and Alex for your initial and continued support of my career, to Chris for NaNoWriMo and Alex for the best episodes of Reply All, and to William for the tweet that started it all. Special nod to Catacombs of Terror by Stanley Donwood for additional inspiration.

Special thanks to my friends and family who support me and hype my head: Zayn, Dad, Adam, Alex, Patty (sorry I killed you), Lori, Candace, Dan, Sam, Xander, Chelsea, Jesse, B, Myles, Amy,

Lyndsay, Pinky. If I forgot you on this page, I remembered you in my heart.

Normally, I would thank my twin sister here, but we haven't talked in over a year because she doesn't support my transition. Love, support and affirm your trans family and friends; we need you.

All errors of feral hog facts are mine, and in fact are intentional to suit the story's narrative needs. So don't email me.

About the Author

Dayna Ingram is a trans+queer genre fiction writer from Ohio. He earned his BA in Creative Writing from Antioch College, and his MFA from San Francisco State University. He is the author of EAT YOUR HEART OUT and ALL GOOD CHILDREN, both of which received starred reviews in Publishers Weekly. The latter was also chosen by both Publishers Weekly and Kirkus Reviews Indie as one of the best Science Fiction titles of 2016, and was a finalist for the 2017 Lambda Literary Awards. He lives in the country with his family and their ungodly amount of pets (no hogs...yet).

The Seventh Terrace

Visit us online at
www.the-seventh-terrace.com

Also Available from The Seventh Terrace

Made in United States
North Haven, CT
12 August 2023